From a child, Sharon Vogt, has been uniquely imaginative and creative. Her wild imagination has found many interesting outlets including stained glass, distinctive jeweller designs, abstract art and hand-building pottery. It's no wonder that she retired as an accomplished interior designer. Writing has now become Sharon's passion and she is devoted to giving her readers adventure and romance that will melt even the coldest heart. Sharon lived in New Orleans for twenty-five years, but now resides on the Gulf Coast of Alabama with the love of her life.

I dedicate this book to all the beautiful and resilient people of Louisiana.

Sharon Vogt

DARK WATER SECRETS

AUSTIN MACAULEY PUBLISHERS™

LONDON • CAMBRIDGE • NEW YORK • SHARJAH

A CIP catalogue record for this title is available from the British Library.

ISBN 9781035850495 (Paperback)
ISBN 9781035850501 (Hardback)
ISBN 9781035850525 (ePub e-book)
ISBN 9781035850518 (Audiobook)

www.austinmacauley.com

First Published 2024
Austin Macauley Publishers Ltd®
1 Canada Square
Canary Wharf
London
E14 5AA

My intimate thanks goes to my loving husband, Tim, for his patience and support throughout all the long hours of writing.

With much gratitude, I offer my heartfelt appreciation to Rose Phillips. Your belief in me as a writer instilled the confidence to push through the challenging times.

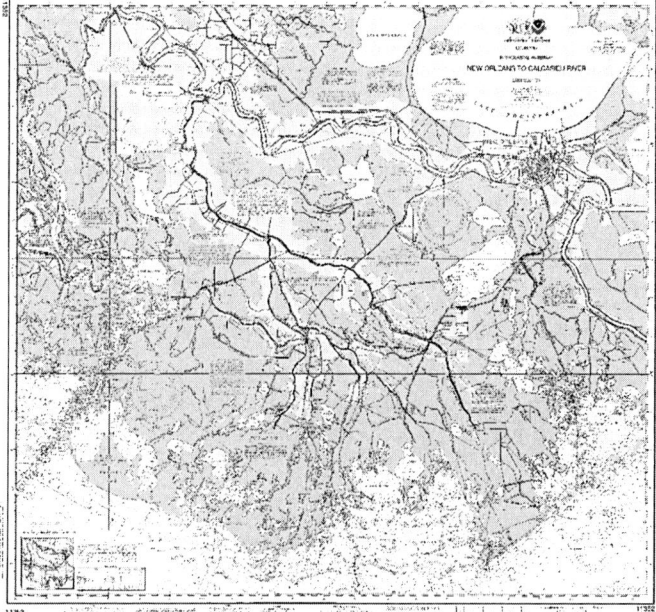

NEW ORLEANS TO CALCASIEU RIVER

Prologue

Evangeline's eyes popped opened abruptly as she woke in a cold sweat and released a terrified gasp. The residual panic from another nightmare caused her breathing to be exaggerated. Paranoia gripped her as she glanced around the room suspicious that the frightening dream had followed her into reality. A man with cold, sightless eyes haunted her dream world. His decaying corpse lying under water was an image she couldn't get out of her head. Evangeline's heart pounded viscously within its ribcage.

She noticed the bedside clock displayed 3:33 a.m. and thought, *Weird! It's always the same time. Whoa! What the hell was that dark shadow that just passed in front of me? My mind must be playing tricks. Help! I need sleep!* Evangeline turned on the light and went to the bathroom to splash cold water on her face. Instead, her bare feet hit the floor and she stepped in water. She rubbed her sleepy eyes and thought, *What's happening? Am I losing my mind?*

The lamp cast a dim glow down the hallway where she noticed wet footprints leading towards the door. She grabbed a towel and quickly wiped up the water, trying to erase the fear that paralyzed and consumed her. Evangeline waited impatiently for the first light of dawn. The weary time between awake and asleep lay before her like an endless frozen tundra. Visibly shaken, Evangeline curled into a fatal position beneath the covers and, like before, she started replaying the whole story over in her mind, like a bad movie.

Chapter One
A Secret Rendezvous

Evangeline's memory of her mother's face was now an obscure image, dulled by the seasons of time. Evangeline remembered playing with a crawdad on the front porch when she heard her papere yell, "Angelle, git on outta here, and good riddance. You can leave but if you think you're taking Evangeline, it'll be over my dead body."

On her way out, Angelle stooped down and whispered into Evangeline's ear, "I promise, my darling, I'll come back for you." Then she stormed off with an old suitcase swinging by her side and vanished.

Evangeline was a child of seven. Trepidation ripped through her as though she had been struck by a bolt of lightning. She cried out, "Maman, please don't go. Please don't leave me here." Ten years later, that recollection still haunted her. During quiet times, she sometimes pondered, *Maman, why did you leave me? What did I do that made you not love me anymore? You said you would come back for me!*

Left to fend mostly for herself, Evangeline became a child of the Louisiana swamps—setting traps and fishing for her food.

With a limited education, her papere did the only thing he knew—he worked on a shrimp boat. On his off days, he drank and gambled his earnings. Most times, he lost playing cards, which made him a volatile drunk and totally unreliable. Such was life for a young abandoned girl, but destiny had another plan.

After Angelle's departure, fear and anger had boiled inside Evangeline until finally, there was nothing left but a peevish simmer. After months of grieving, she decided to turn that energy into a positive tool for survival. She unceremoniously laid her maman's ghost to rest, allowing for peace and the blessed balm of forgiveness to enter her heart.

Evangeline's school in Lafitte became a safe place where she sought refuge. Arriving early and staying late, she soaked up knowledge as though she were a sponge. One particular teacher, Mr. Stonicher, took notice and encouraged Evangeline as she continued to exhibit a keen intelligence. Finally, the happy day came when she walked across the stage and received her high-school diploma with honours.

While fellow graduates of the class of 1969 celebrated with a big party, Evangeline lay curled up on her saggy mattress alone. A light salty breeze from the Gulf of Mexico drifted through the bedroom window bearing the scent of magnolia blossoms. The clamorous croaking of frogs, and the rumbling bellow of a gator created a soothing nocturnal chorus. The night air was sultry and humid, yet in the Gulf of Mexico, an early tropical storm steadily churned its way towards the coastline.

Earlier in the evening, Evangeline had poured her abusive papere ample servings of whiskey with the intention of inebriating him. She had plans to meet her beloved, Jean-

Baptiste, to celebrate graduation in her own style. She boiled shrimp and scored a six-pack of Dixie beer, both stashed in an ice chest in her pirogue. Her intention hadn't worked yet, as she heard grumbling and rummaging coming from the ill-stocked kitchen. Gently, she touched the heart-shaped locket engraved with her name. Inside was a hand-written note, *Evangeline, I love you. Marry me. Jean-Baptiste.* He had given her the necklace as a Christmas present, and she had never taken it off. Absentmindedly, she slid the locket back and forth on its gold chain. Restless, she waited…

Finally, the guttural sound of snoring issued from the other room. Evangeline slipped quietly out her bedroom window and headed to the bayou mere feet from their solitary shack. Quickly braiding her long dark hair, she silently slid her pirogue into the brackish water. She slapped an annoying mosquito before swinging her long tan legs into the vessel. Evangeline loved the mystique of the bayou and admired a yellow-crowned night-heron that was startled into flight. The waxing gibbous moon peeped from behind a cloud casting its silvery light on the dark water. Spanish moss draped like witch's hair from the ancient cypress trees that stood proud, like sentinels along the bank. The scenery, however, was only a back drop to what was really on her mind—her bayou boy.

Evangeline loved to run her fingers through Jean-Baptiste's thick, dark hair that spilled to his shoulders. Tall and statuesque with defined muscles, he possessed piercing, arctic blue eyes. Giddy and tingling with the thought of him, she felt an unprecedented level of excitement. Evangeline's forward stroke became purposeful. She must hurry…

While paddling through the mysterious bayou, Evangeline's mind wondered to the streets of the French

14

Quarter, the historic heart of New Orleans. She could almost hear the hypnotic rhythm of jazz drifting over the foggy Mississippi River and smell the Confederate Jasmine that clung to the wrought iron balconies of the Corn Stalk Hotel. The fragrant blooms wafted their sweet-smelling essence on the current of a humid breeze. Evangeline and Jean-Baptiste had plans to marry and move to the French Quarter after her graduation. Presently, they lacked the funds to realize their dream. Jean-Baptiste graduated high school the year before and got a job working on a shrimp boat. He assured Evangeline that he had devised a plan and soon they would have enough money to leave.

As she approached their secret rendezvous place, panic fluttered in her soul like a trapped bird. Not a single candle burned in the decaying old shack to welcome her. Jean-Baptiste was always there waiting, until tonight. She knew deep in her heart that something serious must have happened.

Chapter Two
All or Nothing

Jean-Baptiste lost the last hand of poker and pondered his next move. He thought, *This next round is an all or nothing gamble. Luck, please be a lady tonight.* The dealer took a big draw off his hand-rolled stogie and dealt five cards to the seven players. A rusty ceiling fan complained noisily while making its repetitive orbit and swirling pungent smoke throughout the musty room.

Holding two kings, Jean-Baptiste confidently asked for three more cards. Trying to maintain a poker face, he smiled inwardly after receiving another king and a wild joker. Gambling his last two pay checks from the shrimp boats had left him worse off, but tonight's winnings could give him and Evangeline the cash needed to escape to New Orleans. Jean-Baptiste had a feeling that tonight his luck would change for the better.

The barmaid dropped a quarter into the juke box and "Bad Moon Rising" by Creedence Clearwater Revival reverberated off the walls. Jean-Baptiste hummed along, and raised the bet with a well-timed bluff. He fumbled with the corners of the cards, took a sip of whiskey and said, "All in, call." The other players sniggered at his youth and naivete, but three of them folded. The pot had increased substantially yet nobody called, so it went into a showdown. With all hands down, Jean-Baptiste was easily the winner. Grumblings and threats ensued as he pocketed his winnings and headed for the door. "Thanks a lot, boys! I'd love to hang out with you muskrats but I've got a hot date with a beautiful girl. See ya around!"

While making his getaway he was thinking, *I'm late, but I can't wait to see Evangeline. She's gonna be so surprised with her graduation present. Damn it, as soon as I can, I'm putting a ring on that girl's finger.*

As Jean-Baptiste made his way to the skiff, two men jumped from the shadow of a live oak tree and tackled him. He fought them gallantly until one of the men hit him on the head with a shovel, triggering a blackout. The thieves relieved him of his winnings and his skiff, dumped him in the bayou and left him there to die. Jean-Baptiste's blood pooled and swirled in the water. An alligator's smell is so acute they can detect a single drop of blood in ten gallons of water. The bandits counted on the gators to clean up their messy evidence. With sinister laughter, the marauders sped away, leaving Jean-Baptiste floating face down in the bayou.

Chapter Three
A Dreadful Feeling

Evangeline lit two candles and the flames danced to life, casting ghostly shadows in the godforsaken shack of their secret place. She paced like a caged animal in a state of suspense and anxiety, wondering what had happened to Jean-Baptiste. She felt uneasy as a shiver of fear trickled down her spine. In her heart, she knew that he wasn't coming. She could not shake the feeling that something dreadful had happened.

A thunderous crash boomed loudly as something heavy slammed onto the shack. A startled animal scurried across the floor, probably a racoon. Evangeline recoiled from fright and fought a rising panic. Usually, she was never one to be fearful, but tonight she felt alone and vulnerable with a degree of mental uncertainty. Blowing out the candles, she left the shack with a worried feeling that covered her like a damp blanket. She quickly made her way to the pirogue and noticed that a huge limb from a magnolia tree had fallen onto the shack. She laughed at her imagination gone wild, but it didn't help lift her spirits.

Salty tears of disappointment escaped down Evangeline's cheeks. She secured the pirogue to the ancient oak in her front yard, hopeful that her papere would still be in a drunken stupor. She wanted to lie in bed and escape this feeling of doom that would not leave her. The comforting sounds of crickets performing their night-time symphony filled the humid air with a deceptive sense of normalcy. Evangeline quietly tiptoed up the steps, still musing about what could have happened to Jean-Baptiste. She was caught unaware when suddenly, from the darkness, her papere yelled, "Know anybody wantin' in? Come mere, you little slut."

She trembled when he grabbed her long hair and vehemently swung her around. He hit her viciously across the face. "Where have ya been? Who ya been with? And dontcha dare lie to me. You ain't no betta than yo whoring maman that left us here to rot." He drew back his thick ham of a hand and punched Evangeline again, knocking her down. She saw stars as a sharp pain ricocheted through her head.

"Stop!" she shouted through the throbbing pain. "I haven't been with anyone. I couldn't sleep and only went for a paddle on this moonlit night. Please, Papere, let me fix you a drink of whiskey."

He pulled Evangeline to him and sniffed her like a dog, "Get yo lying ass inside. Dis ain't over. I'm gonna put a stop to yo sneaking around."

Quickly, she ran into the shack and grabbed the cast iron skillet hanging from a nail in the makeshift kitchen. Evangeline hid behind the door—and waited. She heard her papere driving nails into her window with a hammer. When he stumbled across the threshold, a fury like she had never felt exploded inside her. With all her might, she swung the heavy skillet, hitting him directly in the face. Shock registered in his bloodshot eyes as he teetered unsteadily on his feet.

Evangeline swung again, making direct contact with his surprised face.

Without uttering a single word, he lurched towards her and grabbed her around the neck. He faltered and she seized the opportunity and pushed him hard. He fell backwards with a heavy thud. Evangeline screamed, releasing the last of her rage, "You will never hit me again, you miserable old man." She was trembling and felt her heart beating wildly against her ribcage. The skillet fell out of her hand, landing hard on the floor, producing a cacophony of discordant sound waves.

Evangeline felt numb and disembodied as though she were another person observing the surreal scene. She expected her papere to get up at any minute and give her a thrashing, but he did not move. Upon closer inspection, she realized he was no longer breathing.

Chapter Four
Guardian of a Secret

Jean-Baptiste opened his swollen eyes slowly and his head throbbed intently. He lay on an uncomfortable cot in a very strange place. A mortar and pestle had recently been used. The smells of crushed herbs permeated the room. Various plants hung withered from the rafters and an assortment of dried toads and insects filled a glass bowl. He noticed an altar with star quartz crystals and various bones. Candles flickered while sage wafted its herbaceous fragrance. He thought, *Is this a witch's lair? How the hell did I get here?*

As Jean-Baptiste slowly recaptured his wits, a creature that seemed to be part human and certainly all swamp came gliding through the door. Jean-Baptiste gasped. Her presence disturbed him. He thought, *I can hear her tattered dress dragging across the plank floor, but it looks like she's floating? How is that possible?*

The witch's long, mossy hair hung down over her raggedy clothes. She laughed hysterically and her eyes seemed to glow or shimmer. The old crone let out a whistle between her missing teeth and gave Jean-Baptiste a wicked grin. She hunched over him. Rubbing her hands together, she let out a mischievous childlike chuckle. The rancid smell of her breath assaulted him. Flicking her tongue like a snake, she spoke in a crackly voice, "I'm Swamp Witch Haddie. I 'appen to be comin' by in me pirogue and seen what dem men did. I brung ya here. You been out of it for twee days, but you better now, huh? Dat storm blew thru causing chaos, but we survived jest fine."

Jean-Baptiste forced a smile at Swamp Witch Haddie. "Thank you, Haddie. You saved my life, and I'm forever in your debt."

She grinned. "Ah! No need fo dat. I gots to tell you sumtin. I been protecting a secret dats been buried in mystery fo years. Many moons men have hunted it, but dey all fail. Jean-Baptiste, I see dat you got a good soul."

He gasped and interrupted, "How do you know my name?"

The witch grinned a toothless smile. "I know many things. I'm a seer and I have seen yo Evangeline. A terrible thang done happened and she run away. Soon she gonna be taking a big voyage across the seas, but if you hurry, you'll find her in the most obvious place of your dreams."

Jean-Baptiste anxiously replied, "You know where she's at? Please tell me now; tell me now, old woman."

Swamp Witch Haddie ignored him and patiently stirred her mysterious concoction while humming. She dipped a cup and handed it to him. "Drink dis and you'll have the gift of sight and understanding."

Jean-Baptiste choked as he drank the ill-tasting brew and watched the witch with curiosity. She clumsily dragged a rickety table to the side and flipped back an old grass rug. Stooping vicariously, she removed two loose boards from the floor and retrieved an ornate bronze box. She swayed

22

hypnotically and chanted while shaking a turtle rattle. With a hammer, she struck the lock with great force. Inside was a bag of old coins, along with a brilliant sapphire and a tattered old map.

"Dis map show where Jean Lafitte buried a large cache of treasure. My great-grandmother was originally charged with protecting this map, now I'm the last living soul that knows bout dis. I'm a tired and lonely old hag and my time is short. Now go find Evangeline, den locate the treasure. Promise me dis, Jean-Baptiste. Release me from dis burdensome secret. Go live a beautiful life far from here."

He asked, "Why didn't you seek the treasure, Haddie*?"*

She chuckled and replied, "What use do I have of treasure? Dis bayou has been my treasure. Now go. You haven't much time. Take my Creole skiff, cause I on't be needing it any mo. Here, I got a little cash, take dat too. You gonna need it."

Jean-Baptiste said, "I'm forever indebted to you, Haddie. I don't know how to thank you. Perhaps one day I'll find a way to honour you. Many blessings, Haddie. You're a kind soul." He bowed to her and left with the loot securely tucked inside an old leather bag.

Swamp Witch Haddie watched Jean-Baptiste leave and peace descended upon her. She smiled and took one last breath. Glowing lights like fireflies hovered over her body and escorted her soul out the window to another dimension.

Chapter Five
Regrets Be Damned

Evangeline came to her senses and realized the gravity of her situation. Instinct kicked in and she flew into action, wrapping her papere in an old sheet. The heavy corpse thumped as she drug it off the porch, feet-first down the steps, and rolled him into the pirogue. She retrieved a heavy anvil from the shed and secured it to the body with old fishing net. Evangeline ran inside and grabbed a few things including the family pistol, a jar of coins and what little clothing she owned. Looking around the humble room, she picked up the skillet too, as an afterthought. She heard the VHF crackle and a voice issued forth a warning to take necessary precautions because Tropical Storm Albert was gaining intensity with the possibility of turning into a hurricane.

Evangeline tied the pirogue behind her papere's old skiff. She pulled hard on the outboard motor starter cord. It stuttered and stalled. She tried again, to no avail. The strong smell of gasoline indicated that Evangeline had flooded the engine. The predawn sky turned a scarlet red. *Not a good omen*, she surmised. There wasn't much time; she had to hurry. Evangeline pulled on the cord again and the old mercury sputtered to life. She released the lines and headed towards the main pass.

The wind picked up, blowing a good twenty-five knots. Goosebumps formed on her bare arms as the tempestuous gale assaulted her. Evangeline guided the skiffs into a secluded inlet. The indigo iris were still blooming, creating a sense of reverence and mystery in the omnipresent swamp. Locust, water hickory, and tupelo trees accompanied the bald cypress. A jewel-bright damselfly tenaciously anchored itself onto a reed while a water moccasin slithered silently through the undergrowth hunting for frogs.

This place is perfect, she thought. *The marsh ferns and palmettoes create a private enclave to protect my secret.* Evangeline pulled the pirogue alongside and fired three shots into its floor. Thunderous soundwaves resonated throughout the eerie-morning and all the birds took flight. Water immediately rushed into the holes and she watched as her papere sank slowly to his final resting place. The last air bubble escaped from the pirogue as it settled into the thick mud. Evangeline tried not to think about the gators that would soon come. With a tear-stained face, she spoke softly, "Goodbye Papere! I release your body back to Mother Nature. May she cleanse your soul and forgive you as I do now. I'm sorry it had to end this way. Peace and forgiveness be with you and me."

Evangeline's thoughts immediately turned to Jean-Baptiste. *Where are you, my love?* She released a sigh, cranked the engine and headed towards Gaston's Shrimp Fleet. Storming into the office, she asked anxiously, "Gaston, have you seen Jean-Baptiste?"

"Hell no! Dat bastard didn't show up for work. Sumbody said he won the jackpot playing poker, but nobody's seen hide nor hair of him since. One of the guys said he was headed to get 'em one of dem expensive French Quarter call girls. If you see 'em though, tell 'em he's fired. Girl, you too good for the likes of dat one. Now go home, we've gotta secure these boats before dat storm gits here."

Evangeline's concern turned to doubt and betrayal. *Damn you, Jean-Baptiste. How could you do this to us?* When she left the no-wake zone, the heavens opened and a deluge of stinging rain assaulted her. Twisting the throttle wide open, she put her head down low and turned into the wind. With not much more than a pocket full of dreams, she headed towards New Orleans and never once looked back. Regrets be damned.

Chapter Six
The Place of Dreams

Jean-Baptiste left the witch's secluded shack and poled his way through the thick alligator and oyster grass before cranking the engine. He had always prided himself on knowing all the confusing Louisiana waterways, but everything looked unfamiliar and he became disoriented until Bayou Verret emptied into Lake Cataouatche. Then he became cognizant of his heading. He sped across the lake and came upon a channel leading into Lake Salvador. He twisted the throttle and headed across the lake to Evangeline's house. Her papere's skiff and her pirogue were both gone. He yelled, "Evangeline! Evangeline! Where are you?" There was no answer. He stepped inside and didn't notice anything out of the ordinary. *Haddie must have been right, but what happened to make her flee without me?*

Jean-Baptiste took the pass at Bayou Villars and cruised into the Barataria Waterway that eventually led to the Harvey Canal. He was on the way to New Orleans, the place of his dreams. An overgrowth of hyacinth, also known as bayou orchids, forced him to idle down. Their long tendrils were infamous for wrapping around a propeller and stranding a boater. The morning sun came out and burned off the last of the fog and the low-lying clouds. A beautiful pair of white egrets rose in a graceful flight. Gulls and terns were circling what was no doubt a shrimp boat on the lake just to the west. He took a moment to appreciate the pleasing sight while easing through the congested area and on towards the Harvey Canal.

Jean-Baptiste made it through the industrial section of the canal and tortoise-like he slowed down while approaching the Harvey Locks. He called up the lock master on VHF14 who informed him he would have to wait as a large tug was in the process of passing through. While he waited, he recalled the history of this canal. Its earlier roots dated back to the French colonial period of Louisiana.

Jean-Baptiste Destrehan and other French men began digging canals in the early 1700s. In 1848, the Harvey family acquired the canal, but before 1907, it was not connected to the river. Passengers from New Orleans would have to walk across the levy to board a steamboat. This famous canal and lock have served the trade and commerce industry for many years. It's an important gateway between the Mississippi River and the swamps and bayous.

After forty-five minutes, Jean-Baptiste eased into the locks and the gates closed behind him. Water boiled around the skiff until finding its equilibrium. Then the locks opened emptying him into the mighty Mississippi. Checking for river traffic, he sped across the great expanse. As he plowed his way against the strong current, waves splashed and spilled into the shallow skiff. He hugged the shoreline of the east bank until he came to Governor Nichols Wharf and secured the witch's old skiff to a piling. An elder black man holding a cane fishing pole appraised the scene warily. Jean-Baptiste cautiously approached the old man and said, "Sir, how would you like to have that old skiff there?"

With all smiles, the man replied, "Yes sir! I'm Willie John. Thank you, man. You just made by day. Now dats alright."

Jean-Baptiste said goodbye to Willie and hurriedly crossed the railroad tracks into the French Quarter. Torrential rain from the storm had caused tremendous flooding. Jean-Baptiste walked through the French Quarter and witnessed people drying out their possessions and trying to get back to something that resembled normal.

The rowdy sounds of *Honkey Tonk Woman* spilled out into the street. Jean-Baptiste entered Ruby Red's Bar and Hamburger Joint, crunching peanut shells beneath his boots and took a seat at the bar. The aromatic smells of hamburgers and onions on the grill made him realize that he was beyond hungry. Jean-Baptist ordered a hamburger with all the fixings and a beer. Quickly, he said, "Please, if it's not too late, make it a cheeseburger?" The bartender nodded and Jean-Baptiste showed him a photo of Evangeline. "Have you seen this beautiful lady lately?"

The bartender smiled and shook his head. "Nope" was all he said.

Chapter Seven
A Powerful Tide

Evangeline shivered from the cold and pelting rain. The wind howled relentlessly, and the sky had become dark and oppressive. She could barely feel her fingers as she gripped the throttle tight. Her core body temperature was dropping. Visibility was an issue putting her at a greater risk. Then the unthinkable happened. The engine sputtered once, twice and went dead. Not wanting to accept the inevitable, she tried desperately to restart the engine. Out of gasoline and floating hopelessly, tears formed in her blue eyes. *Jean-Baptiste, I'm so angry at you right now! How could you have done this to me?*

Five short blasts from an oil rig supply boat snapped her back to reality. The large vessel passed mere feet of her and the huge wake swamped her boat. Evangeline went overboard with no lifejacket and the skiff was sinking. A deckhand on the stern saw her go under, and ran to the captain. He immediately turned on the searchlights and reduced the speed to idle. Slowly, he turned the vessel to the portside. A crew member threw a rope ladder over the railing along with a lifebuoy.

When Evangeline breached the surface, she saw the lit vessel floating close by and heard a man yell, "Grab the lifebuoy! Hang on tight, I'll pull you in." Once her shaking arms were around it, the deckhand pulled her in towards the ladder where two strong hands pulled her to safety.

The captain wrapped a warm blanket around her and brought her inside the cabin. He said, "My God, darling, what in the world are you doing out here by yourself in this weather?"

Evangeline just looked at him with shock in her eyes, too cold and bewildered to answer. The captain instructed the first mate, "Take this young lady below deck and get her some dry clothes and something warm to eat and drink."

Evangeline dressed in a Grateful Dead T-Shirt and an old pair of jeans that were too big. Out of habit, she reached to touch her locket, and realized it was not there. Although disturbing, she reasoned that perhaps it was symbolic of letting Jean-Baptiste go. Everything she had ever loved had left her. Now, she just felt empty, a nobody floating on the edge of saneness. After eating a turkey sandwich and drinking some hot coffee, the shakes started to subside.

She was thinking, *How am I going to explain my situation so the captain won't call the police?* Quite naturally, she wove a tale, "Captain, there were two dangerous men who came by our house saying they aimed to collect a gambling debt. They pointed guns at my papere and then hit him upside the head. Blood was running down his face." Pointing to her own black eyes, she continued, "I tried to help, but one man struck me hard knocking me down. They dragged my papere into their skiff and took off. I couldn't tell if he was alive or dead. I was running for help and ran out of gas."

The captain was thinking there were some holes in her story, but he compassionately replied, "Ma Cher, don't you worry 'bout a thing. We'll take care of this. Is there anywhere I can take you?"

"No sir, I don't have any relatives, that's living anyway. My papere was not a nice man."

"Then you will stay with me and my wife, Rosie, in the French Quarter till we figure this all out. How does that sound?"

Evangeline smiled with gratitude. A powerful tide of energy shifted yet she was unaware that her life was changing drastically in ways she could not comprehend.

Chapter Eight
Gold Doubloons

Jean-Baptiste strolled past the Victorian shotgun houses on Burgundy Street. The distinctive smell of skunky marijuana wafted from an open window as Janis Joplin wailed *Take Another Piece of My Heart* from a cranked-up stereo. A light drizzle of rain descended from sombre grey clouds creating a reflective sheen on the dirty streets. Jean-Baptiste had spent most of the day asking about Evangeline, but to no avail. It seemed as though she had just vanished.

Tired and frustrated, he meandered into The Napoleon House on the corner of Charters and St. Louis and took a seat at the bar. A haunting melody by Beethoven was playing. Jean-Baptiste appreciated the antiquity of the bar and felt somehow suspended in time. On the patinated walls were a sea of quotes touting this as the world's most famous bar. Upon request, Jax the bartender served him a Dixie beer and said, "What port do you hail from, sir?"

Jean-Baptiste chuckled, "Oh, I just come from over ther in the bayou." He pulled out Evangeline's photo and continued, "I'm looking for someone special, have you seen this beautiful girl? Her name is Evangeline."

Jax shook his head and said, "No. Sorry, but check back with me tomorrow. Lots of people come in here, so I'll keep an eye out."

Jean-Baptiste sat in silence sipping the cold beverage and absentmindedly twirled one of Haddie's gold coins through his fingers. A well-dressed gentleman seated two stools over immediately took notice and moved closer. He extended his hand and said, "Hello, I'm Edwin LeRoux, but you can call me Lucky. I couldn't help but notice that coin you have there. Do you mind if I ask where it's from?" He paused. "Forgive me. I'm being rude. I'm a dealer in antiquities. My shop is over on Royal Street. Would you like to take a walk? We can talk in private and you can see my operation."

Jean-Baptiste immediately became guarded. "Oh! This is just an old coin my papere gave me years ago. It ain't worth nuthin'."

"Do you mind if I take a look at it? Son, that coin could be worth a great deal." Lucky pulled his business card out and handed it to Jean-Baptiste before settling the bar tab. "Let's take our leave where it's more private, shall we?"

Horse hooves clopped down the crowded street with their harness bells ringing. It was dusk and purple martins glided effortlessly above the fortune-tellers reading tourists' palms. A short walk to Royal Street and Lucky turned a key on a door that proudly exclaimed, *The Antique Emporium, to Satisfy Your Unique Curiosities.* An impressed Jean-Baptiste eagerly gazed around the shop. "This is amazing. How long have you had this place?"

"About twenty years, but this business has been in my family for over a hundred years. Now, let me take a look at that gold coin."

Lucky stared intently at the coin under a magnifier and then thumbed through a coin catalogue. On page 113 he found the photo and description of the same identical coin.

Lucky said with excitement, "This is a rare French Napoleon Bonaparte 40 franc gold coin from 1806. This coin could have found its way here via Jean Lafitte." Jean-Baptiste looked shocked. Lucky continued, "I'm sure you've heard the stories. Jean Lafitte operated a very lucrative but illegal smuggling operation. After extensive research, I've never found any evidence to validate where the gold doubloons and other treasure were buried. After this many years though, it's doubtful they will ever be found. Do you have any more of these coins?"

Jean-Baptiste scratched his head and tried to be coy, deciding to keep the sapphire for himself. *"*I've a few coins that my papere gave me. I have them here if you would like to take a look."

Lucky replied, "Yes. Please. Let's see what ya got."

Jean-Baptiste opened his old leather bag to retrieve the other coins. In doing so, the edge of the treasure map became visible. Lucky's face lit up and with an excited curiosity, he asked, "Son, do tell, now what have you got there?"

Chapter Nine
Travel the World

Evangeline gasped for a frantic breath, startled from the night terror that consumed her sleep. Her breathing started to normalise as she realized another nightmare had stolen her serenity. Glancing at the bedside clock, she noted the time was 3:33 a.m., always the same. She wondered, *Could that have been the exact time when my papere stopped breathing? This has got to end now.*

Visibly shaken, Evangeline fell down on her knees and spoke out loud, "Papere, I'm so sorry for the way your life turned out. I know you were plagued with loneliness and depression. This made you fearful and mean. You never knew how to deal with your emotions, so you drank to numb the pain. The only problem is, you just created more pain for you and me. It's now time for both of us to forgive each other and for you to pass on into the light. Don't be afraid. Release the hurt and let the healing light come into your heart. I send you love and forgiveness. Farewell, my papere. Now leave me!"

Like a mirage, energy swirled around the room and left expeditiously through the window. Peace and calm came upon Evangeline and she released a long sigh of forgiveness and exhaustion.

The storm had passed and Evangeline settled in at Captain Lafleur and his wife Rosie's Creole cottage on Burgundy Street. The captain had explained, "Sorry, but I'm required to call the police and make an incident report. Don't worry, Evangeline, it's gonna be alright." Officer Richard arrived later that afternoon. He questioned Evangeline and photographed her dark bruises. She repeated her story verbatim. He promised an investigation. "I'll turn this over to the sheriff in Jefferson Parish, but I don't expect any results. The bayou people are usually tight-lipped when it comes to talking to the police against their own kind. I'm sorry you had to go through this, ma cher."

The Captain and Rosie had shown such kindness, yet after three days, Evangeline was restless. She helped with the household chores and two young children, but still felt displaced. Monday morning after preparing a pot of red beans, a realization crept into her brain. *I'm ultimately alone and have nothing. I can't depend on Rosie's compassion and I should never have relied on Jean-Baptiste. Lesson learned! I must find a job quickly and stand on my own two feet.* Evangeline opened *The Times Picayune* newspaper to the employment section of the classifieds. She noticed an advertisement that sent her reeling.

Travel the World

Currently seeking an enthusiastic person for the position of stewardess on the 167' private yacht, Sand Mar Tini. No experience necessary.

Training to be held onboard. Must possess a superior hospitality service to meet the owner's and guest's expectation. Must be willing to commit to undetermined stints of time away. Interviews will be conducted on Friday the 13th at 3:00 p. m.

Location: 1699 Bienville Street Wharf

Evangeline's destiny presented itself. She ran to Rosie who was washing a load of the children's clothing. "Rosie, look at this ad. Can you help me get this job? You and the captain have been so kind to me, but I can't take advantage of your hospitality. Besides, there's nothing for me here, except that I'll miss all of you terribly."

Rosie pushed the button and started the wash cycle. "Evangeline, I think this is a great opportunity. First, let me apply makeup to cover those bruises and then let's get you dressed. I have something you can wear that would be perfect. I want you to walk onto that yacht with confidence as if you own it. As much as I hate to see you go, just know that you will always have a home here, child. It's important that you understand this."

They hugged and Evangeline pulled away with teary eyes. "Rosie, I can never thank you and the captain for all that you've done for me. Y'all literally saved my life in many ways. I will always be eternally grateful."

Rosie gave Evangeline a hankie. "Come on, dry those eyes, girl, and let's get you ready for Bienville Street."

Evangeline approached the exquisitely sleek motor vessel in complete awe. *I've never seen anything so beautiful in my life,* she thought.

She was escorted onboard the 1936 vintage yacht and asked to wait in the salon. Black cherry wood polished to a reflective sheen graced the salon walls. The elegant Art Deco décor proclaimed the elegance of a bygone era. Evangeline stood before a beautiful painting of a stylized yet glamorous woman. She leaned in closer to witness the artist's signature, "Erte". Just being in the elaborately appointed room awoke a yearning inside her soul that she never knew existed.

First Mate Cory Russell called Evangeline into his office. He asked a litany of questions and she answered as confidently as her recent high-school education would allow. After the last person was interviewed, Cory stepped into the salon, "Evangeline Chaisson, please come into my office." He thanked all the other applicants and sent them home.

"Congratulations, Evangeline. You've got the job. This hire is time-sensitive, so I appreciate your being willing to work so quickly with us." He searched through the desk and came out with an employment contract. "Please sign and date here. We'll begin your training promptly at 8:00 a.m. tomorrow and we'll also apply for your travel documents. We sail in three days. Our port of call is Cartagena, Columbia, where the owner, Mr. Wellesley Hyde, will board the vessel. Do you have any questions?"

Evangeline was ecstatic. "No Sir! I'm very excited to start my new life and experience the world. I'll see you in the morning. Thank you, Cory, for this opportunity."

Cory responded, "Before you leave, I would like to show you around and meet the crew." He escorted her to the wheelhouse. "Evangeline, I would like for you to meet our Captain Luis, slash engineer. Captain, this is Evangeline Chaisson, our new stewardess."

"Nice to meet you, Evangeline. Welcome to our team. Should you have any problems, we're here for you. I think you will really enjoy your new job. Welcome aboard."

"Thank you, sir. I'm excited and look forward to working with you."

They made their way through the elegant staterooms and ended up in the galley. "Evangeline, I would like for you to meet the fabulous Chef Jacque. He is the one responsible for keeping everyone onboard in a good mood."

"Nice to meet you, Evangeline. At your service. Happy to have you onboard as part of our small family."

"Happy to meet you, Chef Jacque. I'm sure we will work well together."

He smiled and responded, "Please, we're on first name basis here, just call me Jacque."

Evangeline could hardly contain her excitement as she left the yacht. The thought of being far away from New Orleans would be a relief from the guilt and nightmares that haunted her dreams. She wanted to run to Rosie and when she turned the corner, she did exactly that. "Rosie, Rosie! I got the job. I leave in three days."

Chapter Ten
A Grand Idea

Jean-Baptiste's eyes widened and his mouth gaped open in an instantaneous reaction of surprise. *Oh! No! Lucky saw the map. He seems legit, but can I trust him? I don't have the means to excavate the treasure myself. Lordy, what should I do?* He then looked directly at Lucky who seemed aware of his discomfort. With blind faith, Jean-Baptiste decided to tell the truth. "Lucky, I apologize. I lied about where the coins came from. It's a bizarre story as to how I came into their possession, but I'll tell you everything." He pulled out the map carefully. "This is Jean Lafitte's original treasure map written in his own hand."

They stood speechless and astounded, gazing upon a piece of history that had been lost to the world for years.

Lucky regained his wits and excitedly said, "My God, son, do you realize what this means? You are looking at one of the greatest treasure maps of all times. Of course, I'll need to have it tested for authenticity. If it's the real thing, this map alone is worth a fortune. Jean-Baptiste, we can form a partnership that could make us both wealthy men. This project will no doubt be expensive and challenging." Lucky paused for a moment to catch his breath. "We will need special equipment and we must remain discreet and not call any attention to ourselves. And of course, I'll get my attorney to draw up a contract, to keep it legal. What do you think? Partners?"

With a big smile, Jean-Baptiste extended his hand as acceptance. "I guess they don't call you Lucky for nuthin. Now I'm lucky too. You just got yourself a partner. Ayeee!"

Lucky embraced Jean-Baptiste heartily with a bear hug and then opened a cabinet to expose a well-stocked bar. He pulled out a bottle of Macallan 1926 fine and rare single-malt whiskey along with two Waterford crystal glasses. "I've been saving this fine whiskey for a special occasion and I can't think of anything more special than this moment. This is history and nothing gets me more excited." Lucky opened the fine decorative bottle and poured two glasses. He raised his. "Here's to Swamp Witch Haddie and here's to you, Jean-Baptiste. I salute you! Who'd ever thought that getting robbed would lead to hidden treasure. And here's to a trusting and lucrative partnership. Salute!"

Jean-Baptiste and Lucky sipped the fine whiskey and talked for hours about the synchronicity of events that brought them together. They also discussed how the logistics of such a job could be carried out discreetly. Lucky scribbled away madly trying to determine what equipment they would need and where to get it. Dawn was slowly creeping in edging out the darkness, and the bottle neared empty.

Lucky eagerly flipped through his Rolodex until he found the business card he was searching for. "Jean-Baptiste, I know I'm a little intoxicated, but I've just had a grand idea. Like I said, this treasure hunt is no doubt going to be expensive. I'm not sure how far I can take us, but I have a friend who collects art and ancient artefacts. He has the wealth to finance such a project and I can count on his discretion. Here's his card, would you like for me to call him?"

Jean-Baptiste accepted the card Lucky held out to him. It was like a sixth sense kicked in that allowed him to know something directly without analytic reasoning. He flashed back to what Haddie said when he drank her brew. Somehow, he knew that this person was very important. He smiled and stared intently at the impressive gold font that proudly announced the stately name: Mr. Wellesley Hyde.

Chapter Eleven
Ill Will

Evangeline waved goodbye to the Captain and Rosie from the deck of the Sand Mar Tini. Salty tears of happiness mixed with regret rolled down her young, yet brave face. Captain Luis engaged the bow thruster and gradually eased the yacht off the dock. They were underway, headed down the Mississippi River towards the Gulf of Mexico.

On-the-job training kept Evangeline busy, with so much to learn. She never shied away from hard work though, but rather welcomed it. In the position as stewardess, her duties included the cleanliness of the vessel, waitressing, bartending, crew support and creating solutions for any problems that may arise. Cory stressed that everything must be done with impeccable attention to detail.

While cleaning the crystal stemware, she caught a glimpse of the Chalmette Battlefield as the yacht snaked its way down the mighty river. The Mississippi can be at times a dangerous body of water, but to Evangeline, it represented absolute pure freedom. She was leaving her past behind and on to new adventures. Yesterday is history and tomorrow may be a mystery, but, if you dwell among the shadows of the past, you can quickly lose your way. Evangeline was determined to focus on where she was going instead of where she came from. The past, however, is never far behind.

Scavengers are always out after a hurricane looking for anything salvageable to sell. Armand and Remy were cruising in their airboat doing just that. Armand poked Remy and pointed to an inlet where the bow of an old skiff was visible above the waterline. "Hey, Remy, let's go check dat out, man. Dat storm must have pushed dat boat up on land."

Remy wiped his sweaty brow and eased into the outlet. His clothes were sticky from sweat and the hot moist air. He idled the airboat alongside the partially sunken skiff and Armand jumped into the water. Before each step, he probed the murky water with a stick hoping to deter anything dangerous. A sudden burst of bubbles startled him and he was praying it was not a gator. The source of the bubbles was shortly discovered when the unpleasant smell of death and decaying flesh assaulted his nostrils. No other smell on earth was akin to it.

Armand yelled, "Remy, you ain't gonna believe this shit, man. There's a decomposing body in dat skiff. Holy shit, dats som freaky shit, man. It stinks so bad. Let's get the hell outta here."

Remy picked up the VHF radio instead, "Dis is Airboat Marsh Angel calling for the sheriff's water patrol. Copy?"

Static cracked the airwaves for a few moments. "This is Deputy Benoit, state your problem and location."

"Sir, dis is Remy Fontenot and we done discovered a decomposing body. Our location is Latitude 29.39 and Longitude is -89.94. Copy?"

"Copy that! Hang tight, I'll be there shortly. Don't touch anything."

The deputies arrived and thanked Remy and Armand for alerting them. "We got this, boys. Y'all head on out now and let us do our job. I'm asking for your complete discretion regarding this very delicate matter until the body has been identified. Thanks again, boys."

Remy responded, "Don't worry, sir, we understand."

With ropes and pulleys and great effort, the deputies were finally able to drag the skiff totally onto shore. The smell of the eviscerated decomposing body assailed their senses and Deputy Benoit fought the urge to vomit. The forensic team arrived and started taking gruesome photos of the half-eaten corpse. A shriveled eyeball dangled from its socket. Flashbulbs were popping as evidence was being gathered.

Deputy Benoit approached the corpse thinking, *The dead always leave clues, what does this guy have to say? The autopsy will tell its tale, but looks to me like indisputable proof of ill will.*

Chapter Twelve
Fear Is Temporary,
Regret Is Forever

Jean-Baptiste accepted Lucky's invitation to bunk in the guest carriage house located in the rear of his tropical courtyard. A huge live oak tree spread its branches in a protective gesture providing shade. The flames from gaslight copper lanterns danced and shadows flickered on the banana trees casting a welcome ambiance. Water gurgled and splashed from a tall wrought iron fountain as it cascaded from tier to tier creating a pleasing sound. Jean-Baptiste thought, *This is like walking into another world. I can see me and Evangeline living in a place like this someday.*

Lucky had instructed his secretary, Ethyl, to print a missing person flyer with Evangeline's photo. Fortunately, Jean-Baptiste had one of her graduation photos that had survived the water in his shirt pocket. Lucky encouraged Jean-Baptiste to spend the day posting the flyers while he made calls about salvage excavation. Lucky made several calls and finally contracted a barge. Next, he researched where to find a metal detector and a swamp excavator, the perfect equipment for dredging jobs near water.

Jean-Baptiste grew up going to New Orleans with his family, but he never remembered seeing all the head shops that had popped up selling everything from rolling papers to bongs and patches. He stepped into one shop called "High Times." Burning incense filled the air, and colourful glass mobiles reflected the fluorescent light. A rack of tie-dyed t-shirts stood next to a bin of black light posters of Janis Joplin and Mick Jagger. Jean-Baptiste asked the jovial and high shopkeeper if he could leave a flyer. "Sure, man. Anything to help out a groovy dude." Jean-Baptiste saw a patch he liked and decided to buy it for his blue jean jacket. It said "Fear is Temporary—Regret is Forever."

Jean-Baptiste stapled the last flyer to a power pole. Evangeline was heavy on his mind. Suddenly, he remembered what Swamp Witch Haddie said about Evangeline going on a big voyage across the seas. *Oh! No! Could it be true? Has she left already? Evangeline, where are you?* With a sense of urgency, he started making his way back to Lucky's place on Royal Street. He passed Matassa's Market on Dauphine Street and glanced in the window. What he saw sent a chill trickling down his spine. He stopped, horrified, not believing his own eyes.

WANTED

Evangeline Chaisson for questioning in the murder of Thibaut Chiasson.

Anyone knowing the whereabouts of Ms. Chaisson should report to the New Orleans Police or the Jefferson Parish Sheriff's department immediately.

Jean-Baptiste ripped down the flyer and then retraced his steps, tearing down the ones he had posted. Then he ran straight to see Lucky. When he walked through the door, Lucky said, "Perfect timing. I've got good news. I just got off the phone with Wellesley. His yacht was supposed to be picking him up in Columbia, but after I told him about the map, he's taking the next flight home. He should be here tomorrow. My God, son! What's wrong with you?"

Jean-Baptiste sat down with a sadness that was palatable and handed Lucky the flyer. Lucky already knew how abusive Evangeline's father was, but this was a shock to him as well.

"Jean-Baptiste, don't you worry. We'll find her and hire the best attorney available. Poor darling is probably somewhere alone and scared out of her wits."

"Lucky, she's my everything. I love that girl so much. We have to find her before the police do. Evangeline is my treasure. Without her, nothing else matters."

Chapter Thirteen
Mother Nature's Wrath

Evangeline delighted at watching dolphins race with the yacht while crossing the open water of the Gulf of Mexico. The horizon seemed endless with no land in sight. Although exhilarating, it also felt a bit intimidating. Fortunately, the crossing had been pleasant with favourable weather. The Sand Mar Tini glided past the Yucatan Peninsula and currently sat anchored in the Caratasca Lagoon off the Mosquito Coast of Honduras. In two more days, they would be at their port of call.

After her duties were accomplished, Evangeline retired to her berth to relax. She listened to the constant waves gently slapping against the hull and thought, *I don't ever remember feeling this peaceful. I haven't had a nightmare since I left New Orleans.* She immediately fell into a deep sleep and dreamed of being free and floating weightless over the ocean. At 7:00 a.m., her alarm buzzed and she crawled out of her berth reluctantly. Duty called. It was a picture-perfect day. The azure colour of the ocean was so beautiful it took her breath away. A pleasant ocean breeze blew gently across the deck. Breakfast for the crew had been prepared by Jacque and served by Evangeline on the aft deck. Mesmerized by the sights, she daydreamed about walking on the sandy beach looking for shells. When all her chores were finished, she asked permission to go for a swim and Cory responded, "Sure, go ahead. We have a couple of hours before heaving anchor. The fins and masks are in the aft garage. Hey! give me a minute and I'll go with you."

As Evangeline had never even seen fins and a mask, she mimicked Cory's actions and soon they were in the water. Once conquering the uncertainty of breathing through a snorkel, she relaxed and floated lazily over the reef. A pair of vibrant queen angelfish gracefully fed on giant sponges. A blue tang swam by slowly, showing off its vibrant blue colour. It was a puffer fish that captured her attention, though. She watched it inflate its spiny body with air as a defense mechanism against predators.

She thought, *Sometimes the best defense is a good offence. It's so beautiful here, I could get used to this kind of life. The water is so warm and clear compared to the dark water of the bayous.*

One long blast from the yacht's horn caused Evangeline and Cory to look up and see the captain waving. Posthaste, they abandoned their adventure and started swimming back to the yacht. Once onboard, Captain Luis said, "Attention crew, Mr. Hyde called on the ham radio and instructed us to return to New Orleans. Due to unforeseen circumstances, he will be flying back. Prepare the cabin for immediate departure."

Cory responded, "Captain, I just checked the weather and it looks like we're going to run into a storm."

"Yes, I know, but we've got to go. Batten down the hatches, it's gonna be a rough ride."

Captain Luis led the crew through the safety drills. The main salon and staterooms were secured and the anchor was raised from the bottom of the sea. All doors and hatches were closed. Cory engaged the engines and turned the yacht in a northerly direction.

With work temporarily done, Evangeline found a quiet corner and tried to calm her nerves. Going back to New Orleans was not good news, but she had no choice in the matter. Cory came and sat beside her. "Are you alright? Don't worry about the storm, we'll be fine."

Evangeline smiled. Cory had been so kind to her and she really liked him as a person. "It's not the storm, Cory. I've been through many. I'm just not keen on going back to New Orleans so soon, but I'll be fine."

Cory sensed that Evangeline was running from something. He gave her a concerned smile. "Hopefully, we won't be there long. Enjoy the calm before the storm. It's gonna get a little crazy, but it ain't nothing we can't handle."

By noon, the weather had turned foul. The skies were turning dark as the stormfront approached them. A blustery wind blew and the waves crashed unabated abusing the sleek hull. As the wind increased, the waves seemed insurmountable, like a liquid mountain. Lightning flashed and lit the sky an eerie purple. Captain Luis said, "Crew, we can't run from this storm and we can't go around it. Prepare yourselves, because we're gonna have to push through it."

Then all hell broke loose. Mother Nature seemed to be unleashing all of her wrath. The San Mar Tini pitched and yawed, as the merciless waves pounded her relentlessly. The yacht creaked, moaned and shuddered as the bow crashed into another set of monstrous waves. The crew stared into an empty abyss of darkness as the yacht plunged into another deep trough. Lighting darted unleashed across the grey sky and booming thunder shook their core. For some reason, Evangeline felt no fear. She certainly felt much safer than being exposed in an 18' skiff. As the next set of waves crashed, she thought, *Going back to New Orleans might not be such a bad idea, for I do have unresolved issues there.*

Then, as suddenly as it came, the storm was gone. Where there was rage, there was now an eerie quiet. Captain Luis instructed the crew to check for damages. The storm had blown them a bit off course and they were closer to the shore than the captain felt comfortable. With daylight fading, his main priority was finding a safe place to anchor for the night before making the long gulf crossing.

Chapter Fourteen
Just a Coincidence

Jean-Baptiste was sick with worry about Evangeline. He was oblivious to all the frantic activity regarding the treasure hunt. Consumed with finding her, treasure meant little to him in the moment. Despite his feelings, he prepared for the meeting Lucky had arranged with Mr. Hyde and his attorney. Jean-Baptiste arrived early, anxious to meet this Mr. Hyde. He took a seat in the conference room and noticed an easel that held what looked like a piece of art. He couldn't tell for sure, because it was covered with a sheet. Impatiently, he waited.

Right on time, Lucky's secretary, Ethyl, escorted Mr. Hyde along with his attorney, Mr. B. Morgan, into the conference room. Jean-Baptiste was struck at Mr. Morgan's statue. He thought, *This guy with his long hair and a cowboy hat looks like a modern-day Wild Bill Hickok.* Introductions were made and they were all seated. Lucky led the meeting and periodically asked Jean-Baptiste to interject. Lucky explained that the treasure map had been authenticated. It was in relatively good condition, due to the fact it was made of linen and flax, which is low in acid-producing lignin. He had the map framed with UV glass and used mounting corners and acid-free hinging tape.

Lucky was excited. With great fanfare, he yanked the sheet off to reveal the treasure map. A gasp went around the room. They all stood silent, admiring the beautiful map. Then Mr. Hyde spoke, breaking the silence, "Lucky, this is an unbelievable once in a lifetime opportunity. Count me in."

Attorney Morgan interjected, "Yes, this is quite the find, and an even more interesting story as to how it came to be here. Let's not get ahead of ourselves though." He paused for a drink of water. "The Archaeological Resource Protection Act forbids the excavation of items that are more than 100 years old on public lands without permission. I'll file for a permit keeping our venture legal and aboveboard. Permits are expensive, so most people don't bother. Article 3423 of Louisiana Law provides that the finder acquires ownership immediately upon finding if on private land or with a permit. As far as I can tell, this area is considered public land with no individual ownership recorded."

Lucky responded, "That's great, Wellesley. I was hoping you would say that, and happy to have you onboard too, Mr. Morgan. We want to keep this venture legal to avoid problems down the road. Almost all the excavation equipment has been arranged. The only thing we're waiting for is the permit. In the meantime, we can begin the preliminary work. Gentlemen, we have another important issue to discuss." Lucky asked Jean-Baptiste to explain Evangeline's predicament in detail.

Afterwards, Mr. Morgan said, "Don't you worry, I know the best criminal defense attorney in the whole southeast, and he owes me a big favor. We'll get your sweetheart acquitted. Don't you worry."

Jean-Baptiste breathed a sigh of relief. He glanced at Mr. Hyde, who looked deep in thought, and said, "Mr. Hyde, is everything alright?"

He replied, "I think we should all be on first name basis here. Please, just call me Wellesley. I was just thinking that the name, Evangeline, sounds very familiar. I believe the captain informed me of a new hire on my yacht by the name of Evangeline. It's probably just a coincidence though. Regardless, the Sand Mar Tini will be back in New Orleans soon. I guess we'll find out then."

Chapter Fifteen
Strange and Peculiar

Evangeline busied herself preparing the cabin for the two-day journey across the vast Gulf of Mexico. To their surprise, the Sand Mar Tini had weathered the storm with little damage. It was a beautiful sunny day with only a smattering of wispy, cirrus clouds floating high across the sky. Captain Luis completed the safety check, then started the engine. Cory heaved the anchor and charted a course due north to New Orleans.

The Sand Mar Tini glided hypnotically across the water. Evangeline sat alone on the aft deck staring at the white wake left behind the graceful yacht. Her emotions of excitement and trepidation seemed liquid like the slow rolling swells of the Gulf. She was mesmerized, but her thoughts always returned to Jean-Baptiste. *I have to know what happened. Boy, is he ever going to get a piece of my mind.*

Just the thought of him with another girl filled Evangeline with an incandescent anger. A part of her wanted to believe in him, but she couldn't ignore the hard evidence shared by Gaston. Her mental jousting was interrupted when Cory announced, "Evangeline, Jacque would like your assistance in the galley."

Captain Luis rubbed his bloodshot eyes and informed the crew they were about an hour from the mouth of the Mississippi River. The sun rose, slowly illuminating the darkness. The bright orange ball ascended casting a pyramid of colours from purples to pinks. The mirrored reflection of light made the sky and water appear as one. The Louisiana state bird, a brown pelican, dove head first into the water and flew off with an unsuspecting fish. Evangeline took a moment to admire the beautiful scenery.

Cory took over the helm as Captain Luis went below to grab a couple of winks. The San Mar Tini glided quietly up the Mississippi River in the stillness of the early morning. A low-lying blanket of fog covered the river. An eerie feeling permeated throughout the crew. Even though Evangeline felt awed by the scenery, her instincts were screaming something else entirely, *I don't know what it is, but something seems really strange and peculiar.*

Evangeline stood on the deck as the mystical city of New Orleans came into a distant view. The city seemed to be precariously perched on a lily-pad six feet below sea level. A seemingly impossible place to survive. Yet, her tenacious people embrace the joy of living, making music out of suffering, and naming cocktails after hurricanes. Tennessee Williams once said about the city, "In New Orleans... I found the kind of freedom I had always needed, and the shock of it—against the Puritanism of my nature—has given me a subject, a theme, which I never cease to exploit."

The Sand Mar Tini cautiously approached the Bienville Street wharf. A large crowd had gathered, including New Orleans police, several Jefferson Parish sheriff's deputies, and the media. Flashbulbs were popping instantaneously. A dock worker assisted Cory and Captain Luis in securing the lines as he expertly came alongside the berth. The crew seemed perplexed as to what the fuss was all about. Then a deputy picked up a bullhorn. "Evangeline Chaisson! Please disembark the vessel immediately. You are under arrest for the murder of Thibaut Chaisson."

Shocked, she looked at Cory and he said, "Come, I'll escort you off the yacht. I'm sure this is just a misunderstanding. Don't worry, we'll find out what this is all about."

Cory escorted a shaky Evangeline to the dock where an overweight deputy placed handcuffs on her. "Evangeline Chaisson, you are under arrest for the murder of Thibaut Chiasson. You have the right to remain silent. Anything you say can and will be used against you in a court of law. You have the right to attain legal counsel during questioning. If you cannot afford legal counsel, the court will appoint someone for you. Do you understand your rights as I have read them?"

Chapter Sixteen
A Solemn Promise

Jean-Baptiste stood behind the barricade and watched as Evangeline walked slowly with her head hanging down. The deputy placed handcuffs on her small wrists and then escorted her to a deputy's car. Jean-Baptiste yelled at her, but his voice did not carry over the noise and commotion. Flashbulbs were firing simultaneously, and he knew her photo would be on the front page of the newspaper.

The sight of Evangeline had about brought Jean-Baptiste to his knees. His heart ached when he watched her exit the stunning yacht. She looked frightened yet her face remained stoic. *What thoughts lie behind those sad yet beautiful eyes? Do they confess the secrets of her heart? What has my girl been through? I can't believe she took a job on a yacht. She never ceases to amaze me.* The horror of seeing her handcuffed was about more than he could take. Jean-Baptiste longed to see her and explain everything, but no one but the attorney was allowed to visit her. He wanted nothing more than to hold her, and console her, but that would have to wait for now.

Jean-Baptiste made his way through the crowd as he watched the sheriff's car drive away with his love. He was thinking about the crazy chain of events that led to this moment. Still trying to put the pieces together, he made a solemn promise to Evangeline, *Don't be afraid, my darling, we will get through this together. If only I could see you and share the good news.*

Attorney Morgan held true to his word and hired the best criminal defense attorney in the southeast. Attorney D. Hebert, who always joked that the D stood for "The Defender". A powerful and influential man, he had never lost a criminal case. "No" was not a word in his vocabulary.

Attorney Hebert's staff worked diligently, collecting information and statements regarding Evangeline's preliminary hearing. When Captain Lafleur heard the news, he contacted Attorney Hebert's office immediately and gave a statement as to what had happened on that dreadful day when he rescued Evangeline from the water. "She looked like a pitiful drowned rat with black eyes. It was easy to see that she had been abused."

Attorney Hebert searched for witnesses that would discredit Thibaut Chiasson's ability as a father. It seemed that no one in the bayou would willingly come forward to testify. He would have to issue a subpoena ad testificandum for the reluctant witnesses. The first person he wanted to talk with was Thibaut's employer. Attorney Hebert prided himself on always having one surprise witness that would help turn the case around. Right now, he did not have that witness in his arsenal, and that was troubling.

Chapter Seventeen
Rotten and No Good

Evangeline cooperated as the deputy collected her personal information. He cleaned each of her fingers with alcohol and roughly rolled each finger on an ink blot. Then he transferred the ink onto a prepared card. The deputy said sarcastically, "So, you killed your old man, huh? I ain't got nothing for a killer."

Evangeline remained silent. After being photographed and processed the deputy placed her in a holding cell. All the other officers whistled and made lewd remarks towards her as she endured their humiliation. No place to hide. She was determined to hold back the tears and not let them see how angry and afraid she really was. *How did this happen? I don't understand. How did they find out? Jean-Baptiste, where are you? I'm so angry with you.*

A deputy escorted Evangeline into an interrogation room. She sat down on an institutional styled chair beside a dented metal table and waited. The bright lights and cold air-conditioning made the room almost unbearable. After waiting approximately fifteen minutes or so, the door opened and a tall well-dressed man walked in and closed the door. "Hello, Evangeline. I'm Attorney Hebert, and I'm here to help you get out of this miserable place. I have some questions for you, and then I need you to write down a timeline of events to the best of your memory." He paused for a drink of water before continuing, "I have the statement and photos from Officer Richard. Also, Captain Lafleur has given a statement on your behalf. It's obvious that you were abused by your papere and acted in self-defense. Please tell me the truth of what happened in your own words. If I don't know the truth, I can't defend you. Do you understand, Evangeline?"

Evangeline shook her head in agreement. She felt numb and things seemed to be happening in slow motion around her. She looked up at the attorney and with a brave face, slid the pen and paper over and starting writing her story. The truth and nothing but…

Attorney Hebert read her timeline and his heart ached for her. Such a bright and beautiful young lady who had endured so much, yet here she sat in jail being accused of murder.

Evangeline looked at him with sad eyes. "Sir, I can't afford your services, so who hired you?"

"Let's just say you have some very influential friends. In time, my dear, you will know everything. Right now, we have more important things to discuss. Just hang tight and know that I'm your advocate. We must go before the judge tomorrow morning. He will set your bail for release then. Here, Rosie Lafleur sent you a change of clothes. Don't worry, we'll have you out of here tomorrow. Good afternoon, Evangeline. I'll see you at 9:00 a.m. in the courthouse for your initial appearance. I know it seems impossible in this environment, but try to relax and get some rest. You need to look your best tomorrow."

Night-time came and Evangeline was all alone in her cell sobbing and shaking from the frigid air-conditioning. The deputies afforded her no conveniences after she had asked for a simple blanket. She sat in the corner of the hard bunk feeling depressed, yet thinking, *What influential friends?*

A sudden voice from the cell next door distracted her misery. A hand reached around the bars. "Hi! I'm Francine Guidry. What are you in for honey? I got a guilty verdict. I'm being sent off to prison tomorrow for murdering my husband. That no-account rotten bastard got what he deserved, now I guess it's my turn. I have no regrets though."

"Hi! I'm Evangeline, and I'm accused of murdering my father. I think he was the same as your husband, rotten and no good."

Francine chuckled and responded, "Well, good luck, darlin'. I hope you've got a good attorney. The one I had was a piece of crap."

"Seems I do; the thing is I don't know who hired him. Geez! It's freezing in here."

Francine handed a quilt through the bars that she was making for her granddaughter. "Here, honey. Wrap this around you. It'll help keep you warm."

The two detainees passed the night talking and sharing stories. At 6:00 a.m., a deputy came and escorted Francine from her cell. As she passed Evangeline, she gave a quick wink and said, "Be strong, beautiful girl. I'll never forget you."

Chapter Eighteen
A Flight Risk

Jean-Baptiste paced back and forth. His boots made a loud clonking noise that echoed up and down the marble hallway. He was not allowed inside the courtroom; regardless, he wanted to be as close to Evangeline as possible. Attorney Hebert walked up to him and said, "Son, give us all a break and please sit down, would you? You've got to chill out, man. Don't you know that worry is a misuse of imagination?"

Evangeline was alone in her cell when a deputy came for her, placing handcuffs too tightly on her small wrists. The deputy grabbed her arm roughly and escorted her into the chambers. She could feel his grubby fingers digging into her flesh. Evangeline walked with her eyes down, feeling humiliated and violated. She was seated at a table and heard the buzz of voices, like a beehive, rising and falling around her. It meant nothing to her. Her brain was foggy and she could not seem to rise above the depths of her depression.

Attorney Hebert made his grand entrance and sat beside Evangeline. The judge entered and everyone stood. He spoke in a gravelly voice, "Councillors, please approach the bench."

The prosecutor spoke first. "Your honour, I suggest that you deny bail for Evangeline Chaisson. I believe that she is a flight risk, due to the fact that she has fled once already."

Attorney Hebert responded, "Your Honour, with all due respect I can prove that this young lady has been abused. Is the court system going to add to her abuse? I strongly disagree with the prosecutor and ask that you grant her bail."

The judge's hardline history tended to lean towards the state. He reclined in his black leather chair and scratched his head as if pondering the situation. "Due to the fact that the defendant is a flight risk, bail is denied. The preliminary hearing will be scheduled in three days. Dismissed." He stood and exited the chambers. Although disappointed with the bail, Attorney Hebert had to look on the bright side. As slow as the court system moved in Louisiana, having a preliminary hearing in three days was better than normal. He hated that Evangeline would remain in jail until then, but he would make damn well sure that she had scheduled visitations.

Attorney Hebert left the courtroom and advised the eager Jean-Baptiste of what had transpired. "Son, I've got lots of work to do and I suggest you do the same and keep yourself busy. I'm trying to arrange a scheduled visitation for you. I'll let you know as soon as possible. Now, go busy yourself."

After having been searched and processed, Jean-Baptiste was allowed in the jail waiting room for his five o'clock appointment with Evangeline. He was as nervous as a man can be. Finally, a deputy called him back to a stall that was separated between two thick pieces of glass with a phone on both sides.

Jean-Baptiste had seen this scene a thousand times in movies, but this was totally different. It was real. A loud buzzer went off and he looked up in time to see Evangeline being led to the chair opposite him. The deputy uncuffed her and she sat down. The sad look on her face was heartbreaking. They each reached for the phones simultaneously.

"Evangeline, my sweetheart! How are you holding up? I'm so sorry you are here, but we're gonna get you out. Can you talk about what happened?"

Anger flashed across her face and she answered sarcastically, "No, why don't you tell me what happened when you didn't show up the night of my graduation? I heard you won the jackpot and shacked up in the French Quarter with a call girl. Is that true? And who is we?"

"No! My cher! I don't know who told you that but no, that is not true." Jean-Baptiste squirmed in his seat, trying his best to explain. He had only gotten to the point where he won the jackpot when the deputy said, "Time's up."

She shook her head and looked at him with such hurt in her eyes.

"Evangeline, I'll be back tomorrow. Please let me explain. I have so much to tell you. I love you."

"Just let it be, Jean-Baptiste. Don't come back, just let me be."

The deputy came to escort her out and he yelled at the glass, "Evangeline! You know I can't do that," but she did not hear a single word before turning and walking away.

Chapter Nineteen
An Unlikely Reunion

Evangeline was surprised by Rosie's early-morning visit to her cell. Attorney Morgan had arranged her visit to help Evangeline get ready for her preliminary hearing. Rosie said, "Child, I don't have much time, so you need to listen. I know this is a very tough situation you're in, but we need you to be present and aware. Hold your head high and look people in the eye. I have faith that Attorney Hebert is going to get your case dismissed on the grounds of self-defense. Now, let's get you dressed. There's one special boy who will be there waiting for you."

Evangeline gave Rosie a big hug. "If you're referring to Jean-Baptiste, he betrayed me, but Rosie, you're my guardian angel. I can never thank you enough."

"Child, there is so much you don't understand, but right now we need to remain focused. There will be time for that later. We have a big surprise prepared for you, so chin up."

This time, when Evangeline made her entrance into the courtroom, she held her head high. She noticed Jean-Baptiste sitting with a well-dressed man, but quickly averted her gaze. Attorney Hebert entered, looking very distinguished. He was sporting a camel-coloured, double-breasted blazer with a red silk scarf in the left pocket. He smiled at Evangeline as he took a seat beside her. Evangeline returned the smile and for the first time since incarceration, she felt hope alive, fluttering in her soul.

A crowd packed the courtroom as this hearing had attracted a lot of attention. Attorney Hebert felt confident that the judge appointed to this case was more lenient than the previous one. Everyone rose as he entered and hit the gavel. "The preliminary hearing for the State of Louisiana vs Evangeline Chaisson is now in session. Deputy, do you see the alleged perpetrator in this courtroom?"

He pointed. "Yes, your honour, she's sitting at the table to the right wearing a blue dress."

The prosecutor then announced, "Your honour, let the record reflect the deputy has identified the defendant."

The state's prosecutor lead with the opening argument. "Your honour, I ask that you formally introduce exhibit number A-1 into state's evidence." He held it up for all to see. "This locket, engraved with the defendant's name, 'Evangeline', was found in the grasp of the deceased's right hand. The state believes this evidence, along with the fact that the victim was tied down with a heavy anvil, is proof enough that Evangeline Chaisson, intentionally and with malice, did commit murder. The state believes this is sufficient evidence to warrant a trial. That's all, Your Honour."

The judge then asked, "Prosecutor, have you identified the murder weapon, if so, are you in possession of said murder weapon?"

The prosecutor answered, "Your honour, no. We are not in possession of the murder weapon, but according to the autopsy, Mr. Chaisson died from trauma afflicted to his head with a blunt object."

The judge asked Attorney Hebert to present his evidence. He stood, taking his time while buttoning his blazer. He had always believed that practicing law was part theatre and flair, and the pregnant pause always builds suspense. "Your honour, I can prove that Evangeline Chaisson was physically, verbally and mentally abused for many years by the deceased. She lived in fear of a man that should have protected and cared for her. I have a list of witness who will come forward to testify of her abuse, including one of her favourite teachers. However, as my first witness, I would like to call Angelle Chaisson to the stand." Murmurs ran through the courthouse like a tidal wave.

The judge banged the gavel and said, "Order in this court."

Evangeline's breath shuddered. *What is happening? Could that be my maman?* Shock registered on Evangeline's face as she tried to process that information. She turned to see a fragile woman in a wheelchair being rolled down the aisle and to the witness stand. When she was situated in the witness box, a deputy picked up a bible and said, "Please state your name for the court."

"My name is Angelle Chaisson."

The deputy continued, "Place your right hand on the bible and raise your left hand and repeat after me. I swear by Almighty God that the evidence I shall give will be the truth, the whole truth and nothing but the truth."

Angelle replied, "I swear to tell the truth."

Attorney Hebert approached her. "Mrs. Chaisson, would you please be so kind as to tell the court your relationship with the deceased and the accused? Please take your time."

Angelle's eyes landed on Evangeline and a tear escaped down her cheek. "The deceased was my husband and the accused is my daughter."

"Angelle, please tell the court why you left your husband and abandoned your daughter?"

"I left because the deceased was very volatile and drunk most of the time. He beat me merciless. I had a miscarriage because of him." She grabbed a couple of tissues and sat taller in her chair, determined to be there for Evangeline. "I was going to stay with an old friend in Texas City who was going to help me find a job and get back on my feet. I intended to take Evangeline, but Thibaut threatened to kill me if I did. I had all intentions of coming back for her, but I was in a terrible car accident and almost died. Trauma to the head caused the loss of my memory for a long time and I'm paralyzed from the waist down. I've been going through surgeries and physical therapy ever since.

"Not taking Evangeline with me is the biggest regret of my life. Then I think if I had brought her with me, she could be in the same or worse condition as me." Angelle looked directly at Evangeline. "Ma Cher, I hope that you can find it in your heart to forgive me. I can't imagine what you've had to endure at the hands of that maniac. I'm so very sorry, my love."

Attorney Hebert said, "No further questions. Angelle, thank you. You're dismissed." As Angelle rolled back down the aisle, Evangeline jumped up from her chair and ran to her. She threw her arms around her long-lost maman as tears streamed down both their faces. There was not a dry eye in the courtroom. A mother and daughter reunited in an unlikely reunion.

Attorney Morgan approached the judge. "Your honour, my client, Evangeline Chaisson, is a victim of her parents and of her community. Everyone abandoned this young girl. Now, are we, the court system, going to abandon her too? Despite her unusual circumstances, she has excelled in school and has a bright future ahead. Is the court going to deny her the chance of a life that she damn well deserves? Your honour, I don't think it's necessary to call any further witnesses at this time." Attorney Hebert held a photo in front of the judge of Evangeline with black eyes. "Your honour, it's obvious that Ms. Evangeline Chaisson was abused and acted in self-defense. We are prepared to go to trial; however, considering the evidence presented and the fact that the state does not possess a murder weapon, I humbly suggest that these charges be dropped. It's time to let this young lady heal and get on with her life."

The judge took his own pregnant pause. He looked at Evangeline and said, "Ms. Chaisson, do you have any regret or remorse over the death of your papere?"

"Yes, your honour. I am filled with regret, but I have forgiven my papere as well as myself."

"Then, by the power invested in me, I do hereby drop these charges. This case is dismissed."

The courtroom erupted into sheer pandemonium. Attorney Hebert gave Evangeline a big hug. She was laughing and crying at the same time. Jean-Baptiste approached her with tears in his eyes. All the anger in her heart melted away at the sight of him and she fell sobbing into his arms.

Chapter Twenty
Love! Loyalty! Prosperity!

Evangeline rolled her maman outside into the fresh air with Jean-Baptiste by her side. A limo waited out front and Attorney Hebert motioned for them to join him. Jean-Baptiste carefully picked Angelle up and sat her in the back seat. Attorney Hebert instructed the driver to go to Galatoires Restaurant on Bourbon Street. Evangeline sat between her maman and Jean-Baptiste. Overwhelming emotions rolled over her as she held both their hands.

She looked at Attorney Hebert and said, "My defender. You are amazing. From the bottom of my heart, thank you, and thank you for finding my maman. I also appreciate you agreeing to reopen Francine Guidry's case."

The Defender just smiled and said, "Evangeline, the best is yet to come."

The limo pulled up in front of Galatoires and the four of them exited the vehicle. Jean-Baptiste was so gentle and patient with Angelle. He treated her like a deity, and perhaps to him she was. They entered the restaurant and the maître de escorted them to a back room with a closed door. The Defender opened the door to an eruption of cheering. As Evangeline walked into the room, she saw the Captain and

Rosie, the crew of the Sand Mar Tini, and several other people she didn't know. Tears of relief and happiness filled her blue eyes and rolled down her cheeks.

Jean-Baptiste escorted Evangeline to the head of the table and then rolled Angelle beside her. Flutes of champagne were filled and passed around the table. Jean-Baptiste held his glass high for a toast. "Evangeline, ma cher, cheers! This is a happy day. Please let me entertain you with a story. I'll start where I left off the last time I saw you." He passionately began to retell the whole saga about being robbed by thieves, rescued by Swamp Witch Haddie and her entrusting him with the coins and Jean Lafitte's treasure map.

"Call it a fluke, but I met Lucky Leroux at the Napoleon House. He just happens to be a dealer in antiques and artefacts. Lucky, I would love for you to meet the love of my life, Evangeline Chaisson."

Lucky walked over to Evangeline and gave her a big hug. "My darling, it's so nice to finally meet you. Jean-Baptiste has been a lovesick puppy without you. I know this story sounds bizarre, and it is, but it's a beautiful story nonetheless. Girl, we are making, or should I say, discovering history." Lucky looked at Jean-Baptiste and gave him a wink. "This is an exciting discovery no doubt, but perhaps not as exciting as what's about to happen."

Evangeline jumped up from her chair and said, "Excuse me a moment, please," and made a quick exit to the ladies room. She felt overwhelmed and needed a moment to recompose and take it all in. After splashing cold water on her face, she looked in the mirror and reassessed her situation. Her heart expanded as she took in her reflection. *Lady Fortune has smiled on me. Who would I be to not show up at the party?*

With confidence and gratitude, she made her entrance back into the room. A jazz trio was softly playing a George and Ira Gershwin song, "Love is Here to Stay". The tenor sax was strong, yet rich and mellow as it carried the tone with pitch and volume.

Jean-Baptiste asked Evangeline to join him in the middle of the horseshoe-shaped seating arrangement. He signalled for the band to stop playing and then got down on one knee and offered her a gift-wrapped box from his jacket pocket. "Evangeline, love of my life, will you marry me?"

She tore into the ribbons and paper of the small box and gasped at its content. A brilliant sapphire ring set in 18k gold reflected the light. She couldn't stop looking at it. Jean-Baptiste made a noise clearing his throat and she looked at him with love in her eyes. "Yes! Yes, my love. I will be your wife. I'm so sorry, Jean-Baptiste, I should never have doubted you."

He smiled. "I'm so sorry I wasn't there for you. Hopefully, this beautiful ring makes up for that. That sapphire is a gift from Jean-Lafite himself. It represents great love, loyalty and prosperity, and I promise to give you all three." They held each other and swayed hypnotically to the music, oblivious to all the cheering going on around them.

Chapter Twenty-One
Pieces of a Puzzle

Jean-Baptiste looked at Evangeline and saw the fatigue in her eyes. The celebration had gone into the night and it was time to go. Lucky had invited Angelle and Evangeline to stay in his main house. After they were settled, Jean-Baptiste escorted Evangeline out into the rear courtyard. They sat on an old wrought iron bench underneath a live oak tree. He took her hand. "Evangeline, I thought I had lost you, and I don't ever want to feel that way again. As my vow to you, I will love and cherish you for the rest of my days. I just needed to tell you that and give you a goodnight kiss." Their future seemed sealed with a promise. They kissed passionately as the beams of pale moonlight dappled through the branches of the huge oak.

"Jean-Baptiste, I love you too. We have so much to talk about, but I need to see about my maman. But, before I go, just one more of your sweet kisses."

Evangeline helped with Angelle's bath and changed into her pyjamas. They were lying comfortably in bed and Evangeline said, "When someone you love leaves you, the feeling of being abandoned is horrible, yet the feeling of being forgotten is even worse. Maman, I thought you had forgotten about me, but now I know that love never forgets. What happened to you? Please tell me your story, and how come I never heard anything about your family?"

"Oh! I guess it's confession time. Sweet child, when I was only sixteen, I fell in love with a neighbourhood boy. I snuck out one night and met him underneath our favourite tree. Young love can be so foolish and naïve. I ended up pregnant and my family disowned me. I never saw that boy or my family again. You have to know that back then life was very rigid. I ran away to New Orleans and found a rogue doctor who gave me an abortion that I almost didn't survive.

"That decision did not come easy for me, and it's something that I regret to this day. I was so young and immature, but I knew I could barely take care of myself, how could I ever take care of a baby? I know women do it all the time, but once again, I was a coward. I got a job working in a hotel laundry for a couple of years and saved every dime I could get my hands on. Life was extremely difficult back then during the great depression. It really was about survival. I lived in a run-down shotgun house with three other girls. We didn't even have electricity and going to bed hungry was normal.

"I met your papere in 1932, I was only 18 years old. At first, I thought he was my saviour, so I did whatever he wanted. Unfortunately, that was not the case. We left the French Quarter and he brought me to live in that dreadful shack in the bayou where I was mostly alone. Living with your papere was very challenging, but I loved the idea of being a wife and homemaker. I tried really hard to make it work, but one minute, he would be so sweet and endearing, and without warning, his mood would change drastically.

Your papere became an angry man and took his frustrations out on me. He beat me so bad I had a miscarriage and he just walked away and left me lying in a bloody heap on the floor, crying my eyes out.

"You were probably two at the time. I remember picking you up and we both cried together. It's a miracle you survived, but your papere had a soft spot for you. The day I left, I had taken twenty dollars out of his wallet and paid a young neighbour boy to pick me up in his skiff and carry me to New Orleans. My friend Addy and I had been writing each other letters planning my escape. I was going to stay with her in Texas city and get a job so I could come back for you. On the day we planned, she waited for me by the Canal Street ferry. We were so happy to see each other. Then, without looking back, we left Louisiana in the broad daylight.

"We had just crossed the Texas state line, and right before Beaumont, it started storming heavy." Angelle paused, reached for a drink of water and released a big sigh. "Bear with me, this is harder than I thought. I'm not sure exactly what happened, but we hydroplaned off the highway and slammed into a large cypress tree. Blood and glass were everywhere, even embedded in my skin. I was knocked unconscious from a trauma to the head. Of course, back then, there was no such thing as seatbelts. When I woke, I was in a hospital with no memory of where I was or how I got there. The police and doctors kept asking me tons of questions. I couldn't remember anything. They informed me that Addy did not make it. She had been thrown through the windshield." Tears started rolling down Angelle's cheeks and Evangeline hugged her close.

"It's OK, Maman, take your time. Didn't Addy's family try to contact you?"

"Addy was an only child and her parents had died several years earlier. We thought it would be great to help each other, especially since she was recently divorced. I guess both of us were refugees in a way. Since I had lost my memory and didn't have an ID or hardly any money, the authorities didn't know what to do with me. They decided to put me into a state-run mental hospital in Beaumont. I don't think I'll ever be able to talk about the horrors I endured there. I had no contact with the outside world whatsoever. I was literally a prisoner.

"Gradually, little bits of memory started floating to the surface, like pieces of a puzzle. You came to me out of the fog. I started recalling little things about you, writing them all down in a journal. Every day I would spend hours trying to remember you and my life. There are still periods I can't recollect, but for the most part my memory made a decent recovery. Thanks to Attorney Hebert, who found me, I have you back in my life. You can't imagine what a surprise his visit was. He actually signed papers to be my legal guardian; what a nice man."

Angelle paused for a moment while grabbing a tissue. "Evangeline, I love you more than you could ever know. We both have lost so much, but you still have your whole life ahead of you and a wonderful young man who adores you. Please, don't ever feel guilty about what happened to your papere. That hateful man deserved that and more. You are such a brave young woman, having the courage to stand up for yourself and do what I couldn't. I've felt so defenseless my entire life. I let people take advantage of me, thinking I was stuck in situations where I had no power, but you are not like me. You're strong and make me so proud. I know you and Jean-Baptiste haven't set a date yet, but there is nothing that would make me happier than to see you two get married."

With tears in her eyes, Evangeline replied, "Oh! Maman, I'm so sorry for all that you've endured, but I'm so happy to have you back in my life. Please, will you help me plan a wedding? And let's do it soon."

"Of course. That would be grand. Goodnight, my sweet child."

As fatigue took over her tired body, Angelle let go of the tether to consciousness.

Evangeline slipped into the other double bed and felt a chill as she pulled the covers up around her. She released a big sigh and her breath exhaled as a foggy vapor. *That's weird. It's really cold in here,* she thought. Then a mysterious ball of bluish-purple light spread in the mist filling the room with an eerie glow. She could hear a sort of humming or vibration coming from inside the ball of light. *Am I hallucinating? What is happening here?*

The ghost light floated to the foot of Evangeline's bed and turned into an apparition, directly challenging the senses of Evangeline's imagination. Swamp Witch Haddie swirled out of the sphere and smiled a toothless smile. Evangeline froze, afraid to move or even breathe. It wasn't fear that consumed her though, it was more curiosity. Her spiritually open mind intuitively sensed that the witch was trying to share important knowledge. Haddie's voice, which sounded like an echo in a canyon, came reverberating and spiralling out in slow motion.

Evangeline listened as the witch spoke the words, "Nord Dix-sept + Ouest Treize + Sud Onze = Zero", and then she simply evaporated. Evangeline was speechless while thinking, *Did that really just happen? What was the witch trying to tell me? I should write that down. I will in the morning. Oh my! I'm so tired.* Those were her last thoughts before drifting into a deep sleep.

Chapter Twenty-Two
A Celestial Light

Evangeline woke early to help Angelle to the bathroom. "Maman, I had the strangest dream last night, or was it a dream? I don't know. Swamp Witch Haddie appeared and spoke what sounded like French. Geez! I can't exactly remember what she said, but it was very strange. Weird!"

The smell of poached eggs benedict and shrimp and grits wafted into their room. Angelle said, "With all the excitement, it was probably just a dream. Don't worry though, if it's important, you'll remember it. Oh my, does that smell good. I haven't had a decent breakfast in ages. Let's go to the kitchen and see what's cooking."

Lucky had hired a chef to prepare a special brunch for his guests. Evangeline and Angelle came into the bright kitchen where crispy bacon was frying. A large tray of fresh tropical fruits and pastries were laid out on the table. Mimosas flowed from a silver champagne fountain. Louis Armstrong belted the lyrics from a stereo, "The bright blessed day and the dark sacred night..." As Evangeline glanced around the room, Jean-Baptiste smiled at her. Her face lit up and she returned his seductive smile and thought, *Yes! What a wonderful world. I never knew life could be so good.*

The celebratory mood lingered. After much discussion, the wedding plans were all set. Evangeline and Jean-Baptiste decided that an intimate ceremony would be held in Lucky's courtyard on June the 21st.

After everyone enjoyed the delicious brunch, the guys headed out to the excavation site. Angelle asked Evangeline, "Sweetie, would you mind taking me to the St. Louis Cathedral? I know we've never been a religious family, but I would like to light a candle and say a prayer of intention and give thanks."

"Yes, of course, Maman. That would be nice."

While approaching the Cathedral-Basilica of St. Louis King of France, Angelle and Evangeline stopped for a moment to admire the architecture. "Just think, people have worshipped in this sacred space since 1721," Angelle said.

The original church stood for six decades until the Great Fire of New Orleans destroyed it in 1788. The cathedral reopened in December of 1794 and remains a notable landmark of the city. The three spires create a perfect symmetry in balance with the surrounding environment. The largest and middle tower houses the oldest of the bells, 'Victoire' along with a large clock. Three heavy, ornate doors representing the holy trinity welcome all to enter the sanctum.

Angelle and Evangeline entered through the middle door into the vestibule and the bells started tolling to announce the time of day. Angelle rolled her wheelchair to the metal stand that held dozens of candles burning brightly with prayers and intentions. She chose an unlit candle and sat with her head bowed in a silent reverence. Angelle lit the candle and smiled. "Evangeline, life for me has had its challenges, no doubt. There were times I didn't think I could carry on for another day, but that is my past. My future is uncertain, but in this moment, I am filled with so much love and gratitude. If love is what makes living worthwhile, then looking at you right now, child, you have made my life worthwhile."

"Maman, I have missed you so much. I remember when I was just a little girl, you taught me to focus on my breath and meditate instead of screaming out my frustrations. That got me through some really rough times. Let's go sit in the church and just breathe and meditate for a few minutes."

Evangeline rolled Angelle down the aisle and the sacred space seemed awash in a celestial light that came shining through the colourful, stained glass windows. With humility and grace, they sat in silence, and gratitude filled their hearts. After several minutes, Evangeline looked up and said, "Maman, let's go shopping for a wedding dress."

Chapter Twenty-Three
Marred with Mud

Jean-Baptiste appraised the excavation site as the workboat eased alongside the dock. From the coordinates provided on the treasure map, the surveyor identified the dig spot located on swampy Couba Island off Lake Salvador. A sonic readout from the metal detector pin-pointed the exact location. The site had been cleared of all trees and a canal had been dredged to accommodate the barge carrying heavy equipment. Lucky, Wellesley and Jean-Baptiste were greeted by Charlie Dupuis, the head archaeologist and site supervisor. Besides Charlie and his two assistants, the crew consisted of three heavy equipment operators, four diggers, a recorder, a surveyor, two security guards and a photographer.

"Good morning, gentlemen. We have located what seems to be a rather large metal chest that's buried approximately 12 ft. below the surface. I'm sure it wasn't originally buried that deep, but after many storms pushing through it most probably became covered with years of sediment. Our men are in the hole with shovels removing the final layers of mud and muck. With your permission, we are ready to extract the chest," Charlie announced.

Lucky replied, "Folks, this is the moment we've all been waiting for. How exciting! By all means, please proceed."

Digging for something buried in the landscape is like the surgical aspect of archaeology and requires great skill and careful preparation. To locate and excavate the past, can at times be tedious and boring, but today the site was humming with an excited activity. After all the planning, preparation and hard work, Jean Lafitte's treasure that had been buried since the 1800s would soon be raised into the light of day.

The crane operator lifted a lever and pushed a pedal to regulate the speed and direction of the hoist manoeuvre. The beam of the crane sat balanced at the point of support allowing the crane to lift heavier objects with a lesser force. The operator lowered a boom with two straps attached to the men in the hole. They secured the straps beneath the chest and gave a thumbs up. Slowly, the chest started to rise. Once free from the suction of the mud, the metal chest started swinging wildly.

Before the operator could regain equilibrium, the strap on the right side let go. Everyone watched in horror as the chest fell back into the hole and penned a worker's legs. Charlie started yelling orders to resecure the strap and raise the chest off the injured man. Another strap was immediately added and carefully, the crane operator raised the heavy chest and sat it down on the barge with a big thud. Jean-Baptiste held a first-aid certification and, without even a thought, he jumped into the hole to assist the worker who seemed to be going into shock. He yelled up, "We need a stretcher to get this man outta of here, pronto. He's losing a lot of blood. Hurry!"

After much collaboration and team work, the injured man was stabilized and loaded onto the workboat that headed directly to West Jefferson Hospital along with all the team's well wishes.

The chest sat on the dock marred with mud as if an apparition. An awed silence prevailed as the crew all stared and wondered about the contents within. Charlie held out a large bolt cutter and asked, "Who would like to do the honour?"

Lucky accepted, but then passed it to Jean-Baptiste. "I think you deserve this honour, son."

The photographer fired several shots as Jean-Baptiste hoisted the heavy bolt cutters and cut the lock. It dropped unceremoniously as anticipation reached a crescendo. Lucky cleared his throat and said, "Wellesley, would you do the honour of opening the chest?"

He walked over and tried with all his might to open the stuck lid, but time and nature had practically welded it shut. Wellesley wiped the sweat off his brow and grabbed a crow bar. Forcefully, he pried the reluctant lid open. The workers gathered around to witness a piece of history unfolding. The air seemed charged with exhilaration as Wellesley, and Lucky stooped down to inspect the contents. A look of shock and bewilderment registered on their faces and they looked at each other with utter disbelief.

To everyone's dismay and disappointment, Lucky announced, "Damn it! I'm sorry to say that this chest is filled with nothing but rocks. They were most probably used as ballast stones to stabilize an empty ship. I'm afraid Jean Lafitte has pulled a good one. Folks, we've just been duped by a man from another century."

Chapter Twenty-Four
A Mystery to Figure Out

Evangeline and Angelle passed a good time shopping for a wedding dress and experienced a two-hour lunch at Antoine's Restaurant on St Louis Street. Angelle felt fatigued and pain was fogging her mental landscape. Evangeline took her maman back to Lucky's and made her comfortable. Angelle's doctor had prescribed a new drug for her pain, called Fentanyl. Shortly after taking a pill, she fell fast asleep.

Evangeline took the opportunity to try on her wedding dress again. She had purchased the perfect Art Deco, mermaid dress at a vintage shop on Royal Street. She thought of it as timeless elegance, that was plain but sassy. The ivory satin was accented with tiny silver beads and lace cap sleeves with a sweetheart illusion neckline. The back opened into a V-cut lined with a triple row of small pearl beads. Evangeline looked into the full-length mirror and twirled around. Happiness fluttered in her soul like a butterfly. Very soon, she would be a married woman. *Mrs. Jean-Baptiste Landry, I like the sound of that. I always wanted to be a June bride,* she whispered to her reflection.

Evangeline hung her dress in the closet and went to the kitchen thinking, *It would be a nice gesture to have a hot meal waiting for the guys when they return. Mmmm? What can I fix?* She turned on the TV and a news commentor was talking about a 22-year-old man that had sneaked into the wheel pod of a jet parked in Havana and survived a 9-hour flight to Spain despite thin oxygen levels at 29,000 feet. *Desperate people do some crazy things, I should know,* she surmised and turned off the TV and tuned into the Krewe of WTIX 690 on the dial. The DJ announced the number one song at the time and started playing 'Everyday People' by Sly and the Family Stone. She danced around the kitchen singing, "Different strokes for different folks and so on and so on. Ooh, sha sha, we got to live together…"

After perusing the fridge and the pantry, Evangeline removed a pack of shrimp and crab meat from the freezer. She decided to prepare a pot of seafood gumbo with okra along with garlic and French bread. One of her favourite songs came on the radio, 'Crimson and Clover' by Tommy James and the Shondells. She sang along while chopping the holy trinity (celery, onions and bell peppers). *I remember Maman saying that the secret to good gumbo is in the roux. Whoops! I almost forgot to chop the garlic. Whew! That sure is a strong onion,* she thought while wiping tears from her eyes.

The afternoon had slipped quietly away as Angelle took a long nap. Thankfully, the relentless hot sun was beginning to set. It was 7:00 pm and the guys weren't back yet. Evangeline was starting to be concerned when she heard Jean-Baptiste and Lucky come in the back door, stomping dried mud off their boots. She ran to them, excited that they were back. What she saw stopped her in her tracks. Jean-Baptiste and Lucky wore the face of exhaustion and defeat. "What's wrong?" she asked as Jean-Baptiste gave her a light kiss on the cheek.

Lucky poured himself a shot of scotch and sank down in his big chair with a big sigh. "What's wrong is, we excavated the chest and there was nothing inside but ballast rocks. I'm afraid that Jean Lafitte was more ingenious than we ever imagined."

"Oh no! That's certainly not good news. Go clean up and let's talk over dinner," Evangeline suggested.

"That gumbo sure smells good and is just what these two boys need right now. Thanks, ma cher," Jean-Baptiste replied.

Forks clinked against the antique blue fluted china bowls as everyone including Angelle enjoyed Evangeline's gumbo. Afterwards, she cleared the table and grabbed a pen and notebook and started taking notes as their earnest conversation explored all options about the busted treasure hunt. She asked Lucky, "Do you have a copy of the map here that I could look at?"

He presented her with a copy and she looked over it carefully. In the upper right corner, she barely noticed a faded script and took a magnifying glass to get a closer look. Her heart skipped a beat and her hand flew to her mouth. Goosebumps covered her skin and it felt like time was slowing down. Jean-Baptiste saw her reaction and asked, "Evangeline, ma cher, what is it?"

She replied, "Lucky, have you seen this script? Do you know what it means?"

He stepped over and looked at the map. "Yes, we saw that, but no one has any idea. We just don't know the variables that would equal zero. I had a math guy look at it and he ruled out that it was a quadratic equation. Then we thought it might be coordinates but that didn't work out either. Does it mean something to you, Evangeline?"

"This is going to sound crazy, but last night, Swamp Witch Haddie came to me out of a bluish-purple fog. I don't know if it was a vision or a dream, it seemed so real. She repeated these same exact phrases. I had forgotten what they were until I saw them just now. I think Haddie was trying to tell us something."

Lucky added, "Evangeline, at this point, nothing sounds crazy or unbelievable. Just trust your intuition and tell us what you think they mean."

She wrote the letters and numbers down:

"*(Nord Dix-Sept + Quest Treize + Sud Onze = 0)*. I studied a little French in high school and I think it translates into: North 17 + West 13 + South 11 = 0. If it's not an equation or coordinates, then could it be a measurement? But what equals 0?"

"Evangeline, you could be onto something. You're on a roll, keep going," Lucky encouraged.

"Well, we know that the chest you found was a decoy. What if the real chest is buried 17 ft. north, 13 ft. west and 11 ft. south from that location? Could the information provided in the mock equation tell us where the real treasure is buried?"

Angelle had been quietly listening, but decided to add her opinion, "In numerology, zero represents all that is. It's the infinite potential. If what Evangeline suggested is correct, zero could be the proverbial golden egg. The solution to the equation is the location. Zero equals X marks the spot."

"Maman, you are so right. That makes sense. Zero is not nothing, it's everything," Evangeline explained.

"Jean-Baptiste, your girl is not only beautiful, she's brilliant too." Lucky looked at Angelle and smiled. "And it's obvious where she gets it. Angelle and Evangeline, y'all might have very well saved this entire operation."

"I don't know if that's correct, but I've got a warm and fuzzy feeling. I think Swamp Witch Haddie was definitely trying to help us figure out this mystery," Evangeline said excitedly.

Lucky looked at Jean-Baptiste. "I'm going to call Wellesley, but let's not tell anyone about this until we have a chance to check out these measurements with the metal detector."

"I agree, Lucky. Evangeline, my darling, you have breathed new energy into this venture. If you're correct, and I believe that you are, I'm taking you to Paris for our honeymoon."

Chapter Twenty-Five
A Serendipitous Story

Jean-Baptiste and Lucky left the house before dawn, excited to be back on site. The early-morning fog began to lift as the workboat came alongside the dock and the captain killed the noisy engine. Wellesley looked fresh as he waited for them with a thermos of hot coffee. He decided to anchor the Sand Mar Tini close by during the excavation and use it as a home base. "Good morning! What exciting news you two bring me on this beautiful day. Brilliant deduction, I must say."

"You can thank Evangeline and Angelle for this one," Lucky said, after accepting a cup of hot brew.

Jean-Baptiste, Lucky and Wellesley calibrated the measurements and marked the spot with spray paint and a red utility flag. They had indeed gotten a ping from the metal detector, but until verified, it could be anything. Lucky instructed the Forman to begin the process of having the trees and root systems removed within the marked area. Lucky was always a forward thinker and as before he had arranged for the trees to be carried out on a barge. He knew a furniture maker in the French Quarter who could make some nice cypress furniture that would bring a high-dollar value. He hypothesised that owning a piece of furniture that once grew over Jean Lafitte's treasure would be something that people would covet.

Two long days later, the spot of land was cleared. Joe, the heavy equipment operator, gradually moved the tracks of the giant excavator forward into position. He deliberately lowered the cumbersome bucket and the huge claw teeth took the first bite out of the pungent earth. It was a tedious process that required extreme patience. If the chest existed, one false move could destroy it. The last phase of the digging would be completed by hand.

Finally, the diggers were in the hole shovelling dirt and mud in buckets that were then raised, emptied and lowered again. One of the workers used his foot to push the shovel down and hit something hard, producing a sonorous undertone. He immediately took a spade and exposed the corner of an old chest. Wellesley puffed on a pipe when he heard the digger yell, "Hey! Boss, I think we've got something."

Charlie jumped into the hole and immediately starting supervising the excavation. Excitement was in the air and slowly the dome lid of the chest came into view. Cheers erupted as the crew peered anxiously into the hole. Eventually, the total chest was exposed. Taking care not to repeat another tragedy, the large and very heavy metal chest was carefully raised to the surface and placed gently upon the barge. Thoroughly and painstakingly, the crew cleaned off the muck and debris. Lucky surmised that the chest was constructed of an alloy of lead, copper and iron. A very ornate scroll design decorated the elaborate chest and metal handles adorned each side. Three weighty locks stamped with the

Royal Coat of Arms of the United Kingdom secured the chest. Wellesley turned an impressive lock over to reveal the date 1872.

Lucky stood admiring the relic and announced, "People, this is an exciting day that will go down in history. Finally, this is the real treasure we've been looking for. I would like to personally thank each of you for your hard work and dedication." He then motioned for the ice chest of champagne to be brought forth. Corks started popping and the crew began clapping and whistling. It was a moment of celebration.

Wellesley took a sip of cold bubbly and raised his glass. "Cheers! I'm humbled that we have been able to unearth such a treasure. It's not just about what's inside the chest, it's about the antiquity, and the serendipitous story that lives on. Let's remember that if it wasn't for Jean-Baptiste and Swamp Witch Haddie, none of this would be happening."

Jean-Baptiste blushed and before replying he thought, *I wish Evangeline could be here to experience this moment.* "Correction, Sir! If it wasn't for Evangeline, none of this would be happening. I've always heard that something good comes from something bad. I was floating face down in the bayou when Swamp Witch Haddie rescued me. I think all the glory should go to her and her family for protecting this secret for so many years. I've been thinking we should erect a statue and place it on the site as a memorial to Haddie."

"Now, that's a great idea, Jean-Baptiste." Lucky took another sip of cold champagne before continuing, "Alright crew, let's get back to work. These locks are too valuable to cut, so we need to bring the chest back to my place so that a locksmith can open them. Load the chest onto the workboat and I want a security detail to assist in the delivery. The rest of you, start disassembling the camp. We have to leave this place in pristine condition.

"Remember your discretion is of utmost importance. I'm planning a little celebration and all of you will get to view the contents as soon as possible. Good day, gentlemen! Here's to a job well done. Salute!" With that, the chest was carefully loaded onto the boat and the lines were cast off. Jean-Baptiste watched the fan-tailed wake as the camp receded from sight. They were headed home to the Big Easy carrying a treasure trove of history and soon he would be marrying his true love. Like a river, his smile kept getting wider.

Jean-Baptiste, Lucky and Wellesley tried unsuccessfully to open the chest before calling Verne Thibodeaux, a master locksmith. He took his time evaluating the intricacies of the padlocks. He scratched his head and looked up at them with uncertainty on his face. "These locks are made from a heavy brass with the shackle being forged from iron, making them highly weather resistant. Notice the small fish on the back with "Chubb London" stamped on the inside. In the 1800s, Chubb & Sons were the exclusive lock-makers to her majesty, the queen. They were known for their creative and ingenious ideas for security.

"From what I can tell, the locking mechanism seems to be a series of interlocking discs. With no key, however, opening the locks without damage will be almost impossible. I believe the only way is to drill, but I will need a special bit that's coated with titanium nitride to get through this metal. Currently, I don't have one in my arsenal, but I'll check with the hardware stores. If they don't have any, I'll have to order one. It might take a few days."

"Thanks Verne, the sooner the better. I ask that you give this your most urgent priority," Lucky responded.

Chapter Twenty-Six
La Bal De Noce

On the longest day of the year, the florid sun finally faded into magical twilight. The luminous sky over the French Quarter seemed painted in pastel colours not found on any artist's palette. Lanterns flickered from branches of the live oak tree as a sweet incense drifted on the lazy breeze. Decorations of candles, flowers and bows adorned the courtyard while a jazz trio played softly. An intimate group of attendees sat quietly in anticipation of the wedding ceremony. Jean-Baptiste looked handsome in his three-piece vested suit. He smiled while watching a blue dasher dragonfly with wings of green and an iridescent blue body take flight from the old fountain. Evangeline was especially fond of dragonflies and had shared with him their symbolic meaning. *I believe she said they represent love and new beginnings, urging you to live life to its fullest; that's pretty auspicious on this day,* he thought.

Angelle and Rosie assisted Evangeline with hair and makeup and into her beautiful wedding gown. Lucky had arranged for a chilled bottle of champagne for the ladies to enjoy. Angelle held her glass up and a tear escaped down her face. "My child! I have been given the best gift of my life. To see you looking so beautiful and radiant on your wedding day makes my heart sing! And Rosie, thank you so very much for being there for Evangeline when I could not be."

"Angelle, meeting Evangeline and you has been such a blessing in my life. Now, I believe it's time for a wedding. Shall we?"

As if on cue, the jazz trio began playing "When I Fall in Love" by Nat King Cole. Evangeline walked to the upstairs parlour and like a vision, she gracefully descended the outdoor staircase. The train of her satin gown rustled sweetly behind as she stepped down onto the patio where the captain waited to escort her to the fountain. Astounded, Jean-Baptiste could hardly contain himself as he gazed upon Evangeline's radiant beauty. She seemed luminous and his heart thrummed as he embraced his love for her.

The captain ushered Evangeline to Jean-Baptiste and the couple stood arm in arm, facing the Justice of Peace.

"Welcome, ladies and gentlemen. We have gathered here today to unite Evangeline Chaisson and Jean-Baptiste Landry in the sacred act of marriage. The happy couple have written their own vows, so at this time, Evangeline, please state yours."

She looked lovingly into Jean-Baptiste's eyes and slowly released a nervous breath before taking his hand in hers.

"My darling. Until the moment we first met, I always felt like a part of me was missing, but you complete me. You've taught me that I am worthy of love. Many times, I've dreamed of the day we would exchange our vows. I just never could have imagined the events that brought us here today. I promise to navigate this world by your side, enjoying all of life's adventures and comforting you in all of life's challenges. I offer this ring as a symbol of my lifetime commitment to you. May we grow old together in the light of passion, for that is the true magic of love." Evangeline slipped the ring on his finger and concluded, "Jean-Baptiste, on this summer solstice, I do take you as my husband, companion and equal partner in life's journey."

Angelle wiped a tear as it rolled down her face. The Justice of Peace then asked Jean-Baptiste to speak his vows. With a nervous but confident voice, he looked at Evangeline with such love. "Our story began the first day I laid eyes on you. You touched something deep inside me. I was drawn to you like a magnet, powerless against your charms. On the contrary, you did not steal my power, you made me a better and more self-assured man. Your warm and inviting eyes and your mischievous smile softened my tough façade. Today we embark on an amazing adventure. We can plot our course and navigate the life we've dreamed of. I promise to love, protect and take care of you for the remaining days of my life." Jean-Baptiste pulled a gold band out of his pocket and slipped it on her slender finger. "Evangeline, I do take you as my wife, lover and confidant."

The Justice of Peace took both their hands and said, "By the power invested in me, I take pleasure in announcing this divine union. You may now kiss as husband and wife."

After the newly-weds kissed underneath the oak tree, the band performed a lively instrumental version of "You've Made Me So Very Happy" by Blood Sweat and Tears. The dance floor was cleared and the newly-weds held hands and started sashaying around the courtyard. Each guest chose a partner and followed the bride and groom until a circle was complete. Jean-Baptiste pulled Evangeline into the circle and held her close for the *La Bal de Noce,* the wedding dance. The bride and groom danced a waltz starting out slow and then cutting loose as the tempo picked up.

The song and dance concluded with clapping and cheering. Lucky walked to the mic and said, "Bonjour, Mes Amis! As you already know, the bar is open. Our chef is now serving spicy crayfish etouffee, jambalaya, cochon de lait, along with gumbo made from fresh crab meat, shrimp and andouille sausage. Please, enjoy yourselves! Laissez Les Bons Temps Rouller!"

Clifton Chenier, the King of Zydeco, surprised the revellers as he casually strolled into the courtyard followed by his band, The Louisiana Ramblers. Clifton softly played a beautiful accordion accented with mother-of-pearl. "I heard there's a wedding and we came to personally congratulate the bride and groom. Evangeline and Jean-Baptiste, y'all ready for a fais do-do?" Cheers erupted. "Alright then! Let's get this party started."

Clifton started playing "Zydeco Boogaloo" and the crowd went wild and were on their feet dancing. Angelle danced in her chair as happiness radiated from her face. Clifton's music seemed to touch the soul; an intoxicating mixture of Cajun waltz, New Orleans rhythm and blues, and big band jazz. His bluesy, southern Louisiana blend of French, African-American and Native American ushered in a new genre of music, called Zydeco. The good-time music from the heart of Louisiana.

Later in the evening, Lucky approached Evangeline and pinned a one-hundred-dollar bill onto her veil and asked for a dance. This age-old Cajun tradition ensures that the newly-weds will have money to start their new life together. According to her already green-backed covered veil, the lovely couple should have nothing to worry. As Lucky twirled her around the floor, he whispered into her ear, "After this song, go stand by Jean-Baptiste. Wellesley and I have an announcement."

The song finished with a great crescendo and Lucky and Wellesley stepped up to the mic. Lucky dinged his glass to get everyone's attention. "Evangeline and Jean-Baptiste, please come forward." Wellesley handed them an envelope and Lucky continued, "To quote Victor Hugo, 'La vie est fleur dont l'amour est le miel' (Life is a flower, of which love is the honey). But honey is worth nothing without money. So, as a token of our love and appreciation for you newly-weds, please accept this all expenses-paid honeymoon trip to romantic Paris. You will be lodging in the lovely Hotel Da Vinci located steps from the Seine River. Your bags are packed and your plane leaves in three hours."

Evangeline's hand flew to her mouth in complete surprise.

Lucky handed the mic to Wellesley. "Evangeline and Jean-Baptiste, congratulations and best wishes. Have a blast in Paris! We know you decided to delay your honeymoon until after the treasure chest opening, however, your marriage celebration is much more important. It's imperative that you two be here, so we've delayed opening the chest until your return in a week. Then we'll have another celebration. So, I close with a quote from the famous French poet and novelist, Marceline Desbordes-Valmore, *Entre deux coers qui s'aiment, nul besoin de paroles* (Between two hearts in love, no words are needed)."

Cheers erupted and Jean-Baptiste whispered into Evangeline's ear, "Ma Cher, I love you. We're going to Paris."

A 1969 Cadillac Fleetwood limousine waited kerbside to whisk Evangeline and Jean-Baptiste to the Moisant Airport. When Evangeline appeared in her going-away outfit, she threw her bouquet straight to Lucky. It hit him in the chest and fell to the floor. He looked surprised but then picked up the bouquet. He gave her the look of 'who me?' Evangeline just smiled and shook her head as an affirmative.

As the happy couple strolled down the alleyway, they were showered with rice. Throwing rice at weddings is an ancient nuptial tradition that acts as a blessing for fertility and prosperity. Evangeline stooped down and gave Angelle a kiss then waved goodbye to everyone. After sliding into the plush interior of the limo, Evangeline gave Jean-Baptiste a big kiss and said, "Pinch me! I feel like I'm in a fairy tale. You told me you had a plan, but I could never have imagined this. My love, you have made me the happiest woman alive."

Chapter Twenty-Seven
The City of Love

Evangeline and Jean-Baptiste boarded the plane for their first airline trip. After a couple of hours' layover in New York, a stewardess escorted them to their seats for the morning flight to Paris. Gazing out the window of the new Boeing 747, Evangeline said, "Isn't this exciting! We're soaring so high; the thrill is intoxicating."

Jean-Baptiste smiled and took her hand. "Yes, it is, my cher. But I can't wait for the thrill of finally being alone with you."

The adrenaline from the wedding and the excitement of airline travel waned and Evangeline fell asleep with her head on Jean-Baptiste's shoulder. He gazed upon her beautiful face with adoration, until he also succumbed to dreamland. They were aroused from their slumber when the stewardess announced the final approach and descent into the Paris Orly Airport.

Evangeline and Jean-Baptiste checked into the cute boutique hotel and found their room to be small but very cosy and comfortable. He hugged her close and whispered, "Ma Cher, I want our first time to be romantic, so in the meantime, let's go explore this beautiful city. We'll come back about sunset, how does that sound?"

"Yes, somehow this moment doesn't seem the right time; besides, I'm hungry. Let's go find some awesome French cuisine. I can't get over the weather, it's amazing. And the energy of this place is so alive. There's so much history to learn here."

They strolled down the Avenue des Champs-Elysees hand in hand, admiring the elegant architecture.

Evangeline saw a cute sidewalk bistro and said, "Let's eat there. It looks interesting." They took an outside table and the waiter served French onion soup along with fresh baked bread and an assortment of meats and cheeses. For dessert, they chose a flambeed crepe with Grand Marnier and a scoop of vanilla ice cream. "This is so incredibly delicious, I can't believe it," Evangeline said before taking her final bite.

The parks and streets teemed with people enjoying the summer sun. Colourful kites soared in the wind high above the landscape. Sounds from an outdoor music festival reverberated in the air as they stopped to admire a street artist's work. Evangeline picked out a stunning abstract landscape depicting bright rays of sunlight bursting through vivid oranges, yellows and fuchsia-coloured clouds with a dark blue and purple sky. "I love this painting, it speaks to me," Evangeline exclaimed.

After a bit of negotiations, the excited newly-weds purchased the first piece of art for their new home.

Jean-Baptiste had arranged for a bottle of champagne and fancy hors-d'oeuvres to be delivered to their room before sunset. They arrived at the hotel and found a beautiful setting on their balcony table. Impressed, Evangeline started laughing and popped the cork into the street. They feasted on baked brie with honey, escargot and smoked salmon canapes. The sun set low and left the sky aglow with an array of magical colours.

Night-time came and a waxing strawberry moon rose over the Seine River. Jean-Baptiste took Evangeline's hand and led her inside and closed the door on the world. Moonbeams cast enigmatic shadows as he laid her across their bed.

"Ma Cher, we've waited for this moment for a long time. Come, let me show you what love can be," Jean-Baptiste said lovingly. Tuned into her nervousness, he embraced her tenderly and gently kissed her pouty lips. He whispered, "My wife, your love is all that matters to me."

Evangeline surrendered and whispered into his ear, "My heart no longer belongs to me. You are my first love and you will be my last."

After several days of exploring the Eiffel Tower, the Louve and taking a scenic river cruise, Jean-Baptiste looked at Evangeline and said, "Paris is beautiful and has been so much fun, but I'm really homesick. Are you?"

"Yes, I am. My body may be in France, but my heart is in Louisiana. Let's go home, where we belong. I miss Maman and I can't keep from worrying about her. Besides, I know we both are excited about the treasure reveal."

"Evangeline, I love you so much. Yes, you are right about the treasure. I can hardly wait to see what's in that chest. I'll get the concierge to see if he can change our tickets."

The next morning, the honeymooners boarded a plane for the long trip back across the pond. They were going home to their future and a surprise they did not anticipate.

Chapter Twenty-Eight
Pure Absolute Freedom

Evangeline and Jean-Baptiste hailed a taxi at the New Orleans Moisant Airport. A hippy driver asked for the address and drove them to Lucky's. They arrived at the house, only to find no one home. Evangeline yelled, "Maman, where are you?" There was no answer.

"Ma Cher, don't be discouraged. They wouldn't be expecting us today, so perhaps they're out for lunch. I'll call Lucky at his shop and see what's going on," Jean-Baptiste explained.

"Hey, Lucky! We're back a couple of days early. We had a great time, but we were homesick. What? Oh! No! Yes, we will wait here for you."

Evangeline heard the concern in his voice and said, "What was that all about?"

Not wanting to share the news, Jean-Baptiste replied, "Lucky just asked that we wait for him here."

Fifteen minutes later, Lucky walked in the door with a sad face. "What a surprise to see you two back so early. Please come in the living room and have a seat. I'm afraid I have some bad news."

Lucky sat beside Evangeline and took her hand. "My beautiful Evangeline, it is with much regret that I inform you of your maman's passing. She had an advanced lung cancer and wanted her precious time with you to be free from any worries of sickness. I know this news is heartbreaking and traumatic for you. No words can soften the sadness and pain, but you might find comfort knowing that she died peacefully in her sleep.

"After y'all left for the airport, Angelle accepted Rosie's invitation to stay at her house so she could look after her. She went in to check on her the next morning and discovered that Angelle was no longer with us. Rosie said she had never seen anything more peaceful. Angelle actually died with a smile on her face. We didn't want to spoil your honeymoon with the devasting news. Angelle left instructions with Attorney Hebert to be cremated, so that's what we did."

Lucky pulled a letter out of his jacket pocket and handed it to Evangeline. "She also left this letter for you. I'm so very sorry, Evangeline, but what a gift it was to be able to see her again. Just know that she died in peace and was so happy for you. I'll give you two some privacy. If you need anything, I'll be at the shop."

Evangeline collapsed with grief. "No! No! No! This can't be true. I just got her back. Please, I'm not ready to let her go again." Overwhelmed by the news, great sobs racked her body.

Jean-Baptiste held her close and spoke softly, "Ma Cher, Lucky is right. You were given a beautiful gift to see your maman again. What an amazing woman she was. I'm grateful that I got to know her a little. Angelle's love will live forever in our hearts."

"Jean-Baptiste, will you please read the letter for me, because I don't think I can?"

"Of course, I will." He opened the envelope and started to read:

Evangeline, My Sweet Child,

Please don't be sad that I have left this earth. My last days have been the happiest of my life. Seeing the beautiful, smart and fearless young lady you have become has made me so happy.

My biggest regret is having left you. I should have had the courage to stand up to your papere, but fear lived in my heart instead. I was intimidated, and allowed myself to become a victim.

Your papere was not always a bad man. I did love him very much at one time, but alcohol got the best of him and he got the best of me. The positive in this sad story is without him I would not have had you. So, you see, if you look you can always find good in a person. Just know that you were conceived in love. I have forgiven him and I hope you can do the same.

Evangeline, our love has no boundaries. We will always be connected. And when your hair has turned grey and your beautiful family surrounds you, I'll be there waiting when you take your last breath. Long before that happens though, you have a lot of living to do. Plan for the future, but live in the present, and only think of positive experiences from your past.

I adore Jean-Baptiste, he is strong, smart, funny and is going to make a great husband and father. Having a man that can make you laugh is fortunate indeed. I see the way you two look at each other. The love you share gives me hope for the future. I can just imagine what gorgeous babies you'll have together. That thought makes me smile.

Funny thing, most of my life fear kept me paralyzed, yet in this moment, I do not fear death at all. I know my last breath will come soon and I will surrender to the adventure. My last wish is that you cast my ashes by the Canal St Ferry Landing. Perhaps a wrong turn from my past can be righted as my ashes travel down the mighty Mississippi to the Gulf of Mexico. To me, this symbolizes pure absolute freedom. Please play my new favourite song, "And When I Die", by Blood Sweat and Tears. Because when I'm dead and gone, there'll be one child born in our world to carry on. You must carry on, Evangeline.

Farewell, by beautiful daughter. Our paths will cross again. Until then, I leave you with my undying love and eternal gratitude.

Angelle, Your Maman

Wellesley offered the Sand Mar Tini for the ceremony and celebration of Angelle's life. The sleek yacht lay docked next to the Canal Street/Algiers Ferry. News had spread rapidly about the trial and the treasure hunt. A rather large crowd had gathered on the landing holding bouquets of roses, pink carnations and lit candles. Evangeline and Angelle quite unknowingly had become local celebrities. A mother and daughter being reunited was a story everyone talked about. The outpouring of love from the community astounded Evangeline.

Angelle had always loved the mystique of a full moon, so Evangeline decided to have her ritual on June 29th. The full strawberry moon rose high in the night sky casting a pinkish glow on the water. The scene seemed mystical and surreal. A warm breeze blew across the bow and ruffled the papers Evangeline held in her grip. She folded the eulogy and placed it in her pocket deciding to speak from the heart rather than read some well-rehearsed words. She closed her eyes, took a deep breath and released a long sigh before beginning.

"Thank you, everyone, for sharing this intimate moment with me. Today, we honour the life and memory of my maman, Angelle Chaisson. Despite all the hardships and obstacles she endured, her passion for life and her contagious curiosity never wavered. For ten long years, I wondered what had happened to my maman. I yearned for her constantly. Then one day, when I least expected it, she came back into my life. That was a most precious gift and I'm so grateful to have had the opportunity to spend time with her. I will never forget the last time I saw her smiling face."

Evangeline paused a moment to wipe a tear and reflect. "That memory is etched in my mind. She was so happy. This time when Angelle left me, she did so with peace in her heart, as if her life had been fulfilled. I believe our mortal bodies are mere vessels, but our souls are immortal. Maman has shed her damaged body and her spirit has flown free. I miss her badly, but I find comfort in knowing that Angelle's essence is still alive and I will see her again one day. Zero does not equal nothing, zero equals everything and is infinite like the universe. Thanks Lucky, for offering this stunningly beautiful crystal bottle sealed with her ashes inside along with a copy of the letter she left me. My sweet maman, as you requested, I cast your ashes into the mighty Mississippi. That wrong turn you referred to, is now righted. Roll on, sweet angel. I will forever love you. Until we meet again…"

And When I Die by Blood Sweat and Tears started playing loudly across the deck. Jean-Baptiste cast a large wreath overboard of Angelle's favourite flowers—red roses and pink carnations. All the mourners standing on the dock did the same. For a brief moment, the muddy water looked beautiful streaked with reds and pinks bobbing in the moonlight before the raging current swept them away.

Jean-Baptiste placed his arm around Evangeline. Salty tears escaped down her face and she said, "Farewell, Maman. You are now free." The crystal bottle floated eagerly downstream towards the open waters of the Gulf of Mexico, representing pure absolute freedom.